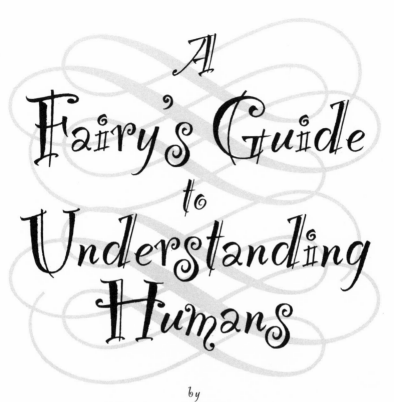

A Fairy's Guide to Understanding Humans

by

Margaret Meacham

Holiday House / New York

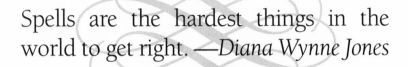

Spells are the hardest things in the world to get right. —*Diana Wynne Jones*

For my mother,
Rachel Marks Redding,
who gave me life, love, and laughter.
See you in the next life, Mum.

Epigraph from *The Magicians of Caprona*, copyright © 1980 by Diana Wynne Jones. First published in the United States in 1980 by Greenwillow Books and reissued in 2001 by Greenwillow Books, an imprint of HarperCollins Publishers. Reprinted by permission of the publisher.

Library of Congress Cataloging-in-Publication Data

Meacham, Margaret, 1952–
A fairy's guide to understanding humans / by Margaret Meacham. — 1st ed.
p. cm.
Summary: Gretta, who is making strides in her fairy godmother training, tries to
help Morgan fit in at her new school as research for a book about her
interactions with humans, but her own boyfriend problems
get in the way.
ISBN-13: 978-0-8234-2078-0 (hardcover)
ISBN-10: 0-8234-2078-7 (hardcover)
[1. Fairies—Fiction. 2. Elves—Fiction. 3. Schools—Fiction. 4. Dating
(Social customs)—Fiction. 5. Humorous stories.] I. Title.
PZ7.M47886Mi 2004
[Fic]—dc22
2006101434

Chapter One

Morgan loved her new room. She loved her new house. She loved her new family, which now included her best friend Sam and his mom, Sally. Last summer when her dad told her he and Sally were getting married, Morgan had been thrilled. For months she had looked forward to when they would all be living together in their new house. She thought it would be terrific, and it was.

Except that she was miserable.

Her dad and Sally had gotten married in October, and they had moved just before Christmas. Everything had been great until January, when she and Sam started their new school, Culver Junior High.

That had been five weeks ago and things had not improved. Morgan hated Culver. She didn't fit in at all, and she hadn't made one friend there. Starting in the middle of the year was impossible. She missed her old school, and she *really* missed her old friends. She talked to Ellen on the phone almost every day, but she hardly ever got to see her.

Morgan was lying on her bed, reading a magazine article called "Beauty Secrets of the Stars," with her green-and-blue-striped quilt tucked around her and Hattie, her basset hound, curled up beside her. It was late afternoon, and outside, a dark purply night was already sticking to the black branches of the maple trees in the backyard.

Morgan knew she should be studying for her English test, and she was just about to get up and go to her desk when she heard Sam shout from upstairs. A minute later he was banging on her door.

"Morgan? It's me. Open up. Quick!"

Morgan put down her magazine. "It's open, Sam. Come on in."

Sam burst into her room and flopped face-down across the bottom of Morgan's bed.

"Sam? What's wrong? Are you okay?"

"I don't know. I think I may be going crazy." He turned onto his side and propped himself up on an elbow. "Have I been acting weird lately?" he asked.

Morgan shrugged. "No more than usual. I mean, you're always kind of weird."

"I know, but I mean, I haven't, like, lost touch with reality or anything, have I?"

Morgan stroked Hattie. "Umm, not that I've noticed. Do you think you've lost touch with reality?"

"I'm not sure, but if I had, I wouldn't know it, would I? That's why I'm asking you."

"Have you started studying for the English test yet?" Morgan asked him.

"Nah. But it won't be a problem. It's not going to be hard."

"Bad news, Sam. You've lost touch with reality."

Sam sat up. "Morgan, I'm serious. Up in my room just now, I thought Marvin talked to me."

"Marvin the robot?"

"Of course Marvin the robot. What other Marvin do we know?"

"So what did he say?" Morgan asked.

"He asked me why I never play with him anymore. And then he said all I ever do is fiddle with my computer."

"Well, he's right about that," Morgan said.

"And then he asked if I was scared of him, and he rolled toward me."

"So? That's nothing new." Morgan shrugged. "Marvin's never done what he was supposed to do."

"No," Sam said. "It's not like before, when his program messed up. This is different. It's like he's *really* talking to me. Of course that's crazy. There's got to be a rational explanation for it. Either that, or I'm crazy."

"You're not crazy, Sam," Morgan told him. "It's probably just, I don't know, a crossed wire or something." She went over to her desk and opened her English text. "Want to quiz each other?" She was glad Sam had come down to talk. He had been so busy with his computer game and his new Tech Club friends that he and Morgan hadn't spent much time together lately.

"Nah. I'm going to call Patrick and James," Sam told her. He stood up and headed toward the door. "They've built three different robots. I'm sure they'll have an explanation."

"Wait, Sam," Morgan said. "Let me see Marvin. Maybe I can help you figure out what's going on with him."

Sam laughed. "Yeah, right, Morg. You know so much about remote-control programming." He bent down to pat Hattie and said, "Remember how scared she used to be of Marvin?"

"Maybe she was right all along," Morgan said.

"Yeah, well, don't worry. I'll call Patrick or James. They understand this stuff." He left her room and ran up the stairs three at a time.

Morgan sighed and lay down on the floor beside Hattie, stroking the dog's long, silky ears. "Even Sam doesn't want to hang out with me anymore, Hattie. He's always too busy with his new friends. And that stupid game of his." Hattie wagged her tail and gave Morgan a soft lick on her cheek. "It's a good thing I have you, isn't it, Hats?"

Later that night, after dinner, Morgan was in her room studying when Sam shouted from upstairs, "Morgan! Come up here. Quick!"

Morgan raced upstairs with Hattie at her heels. Sam was standing in the hall outside his room. "What's up?" Morgan asked.

"Shhh. Listen." He pointed to the closed bathroom door.

Morgan heard water running and then a tinny sort of voice singing, "They said it couldn't be; they said it wasn't me; but I told 'em, yeah I showed 'em. . . ."

Morgan stared. "Is that . . . ?"

Sam nodded slowly. "Marvin," he whispered. "He's rapping. In the shower."

"But Marvin can't rap. Can he?" Morgan asked.

"No. He can't take showers, either." Sam was about to open the bathroom door when his phone rang. "That's probably James. He said he'd call back."

Sam went to his room to get the phone, and that's when Morgan heard it. Laughter. A pure musical sound that floated through the hall like a cool breeze on a hot day. That laughter meant only one thing.

"Gretta?" Morgan said. "Gretta! You're back! I should have known it was you." Morgan opened the bathroom door. The shower was running, but Marvin wasn't in it. He stood motionless, no longer singing. Gretta laughed again.

"Gretta, that was a mean trick to play on Sam," Morgan said, but she laughed, too. "It was pretty funny, though." She looked around. "Where are you?"

There was a pop, and a tiny figure appeared on the edge of the sink. "Zeus, Morgan. This new castle is confusing. Where's your room? Where's my castle?"

"So it's *your* castle now, is it?" Morgan said. When Gretta visited her before, she had lived in the dollhouse Morgan kept in her room. The dollhouse had belonged originally to Morgan's mother, who died in a car accident when Morgan was two years old. It was a beautiful dollhouse with Victorian spires and latticework on the outside and wonderfully detailed miniature furniture inside.

Morgan held out her hand, and Gretta hopped onto it. "It's about time you visited me!"

Morgan said. "I've been wondering when you'd come back."

"Well, you know what it's like at that dungeon they call a school," Gretta said. "The minute we start having any fun at all, they slap some huge project on us."

"I know what you mean. I have tons of work right now, too," Morgan told her, putting the fairy on her shoulder. "My room's downstairs. Come on. I'll show you."

As they passed Sam's room, Morgan heard him on the phone, saying, "Electromagnetic waves. Yeah, that's gotta be it."

Gretta giggled, and Morgan whispered, "Gretta, you're evil! Poor Sam. You really shook him up."

"Here's my new room," she announced, flinging the door open. "What do you think?"

The fairy flew around the room, checking it out. "Great views," she said, hovering in front of the windows. "And look at that nice, big closet! Now that's a real improvement."

Morgan sat down at her desk, and Gretta perched on the edge of Morgan's math book.

"So. How do you like living here?" Gretta

asked. "Is it fun living with Sam and Sally? Tell me everything."

"The house is great, and it's fun living all together. We have a lot more room here. And have you seen the kitchen? It's amazing. Sally loves it. It's great for her catering business. So it's"—Morgan shrugged—"okay, I guess." She sighed and went on, "The thing is, my new school bites. I really miss my old school. I hardly ever get to see Ellen and everyone anymore."

"That's terrible," Gretta said. "What about Ben? Are you two still together?"

Morgan shook her head sadly. "No. We broke up when we moved. We kind of knew we'd never get to see each other."

Gretta nodded. "So. Is there anyone new?"

Morgan frowned. "I wish. The kids at my new school, I don't know, they're just . . . different. I don't really fit in there."

Gretta laughed. "You humans are so dwerg-ish. Of course you fit in. It just takes time. Everyone seems different when you don't know them."

"Yeah. That's what Dad and Sally say." Morgan sighed. "But what's been going on with you? How's Tuti?"

"Tuti's great. And Zeus, is she a wand when it comes to spells. She knows like ten times more than all the Elder Fairies put together. And I don't mean to brag," Gretta said, flipping her thick mane of blonde curls back over her shoulders, "but I hardly ever mess up my spells anymore, well, at least not as much—and I've learned some terrific new stuff."

"Cool," Morgan said.

"But I've just about had it with FGTA. Their rules are absolutely out of control."

FGTA was Gretta's school, Morgan remembered. The letters stood for Fairy Godmother Training Academy. "Really? Like how?"

"Honestly. You know what their newest rule is? We're not allowed to talk on our cell phones during tests!"

Morgan laughed.

"It's true. I swear on my crown. Is that the most ridiculous thing you've ever heard?"

"But Gretta," Morgan said, "we're not even allowed to take our cell phones to school. If we do, they confiscate them."

Gretta rolled her eyes. "Well, human schools.

Everyone knows they're nothing but torture chambers."

"Yeah, well, so how about you? Anyone in the picture boyfriendwise?" Morgan asked.

"Well, there's Bristle." Gretta sighed. "We've been together for a while now. But I've had it with him. He is just way too possessive. He acts like he owns me! So I'm teaching everyone a lesson. I've run away. No one knows where I am. No one except Tuti, of course."

"But, Gretta," Morgan said, "do you really think that's a good idea?"

"It's fine. I'll only stay a week or so. And the best thing is, I can work on my book while I'm here. Did I tell you I'm writing a book?"

"No. That's, uh, great," Morgan said.

"Guess what it's going to be called."

"What?"

"*A Fairy's Guide to Understanding Humans,*" Gretta said, beaming.

"Have you written any of it yet?" Morgan asked.

"Well, I've been concentrating on writing passages in my journal." Gretta rummaged in her bag, pulled out a tiny pair of eyeglasses, and put them on. "You see, Morgan," the fairy went on, looking very serious, "once it's published it will rock the fairy world. I'll be famous, of course, so it's important that I keep up my journal. My public will want to know all about my formative years."

"Oh, right. That's, uh, that's great, Gretta," Morgan said.

"Yes. And being here will be excellent for my research. And of course, I'll have fewer distractions here, so I'm sure I'll make great progress with my book." Gretta fluffed her hair and struck a writerly pose. "By the way, what do you think of my new eyeglasses?" she asked.

Gretta was trying so hard to look serious and scholarly, it was all Morgan could do to keep a straight face. "They make you look very intelligent," she told the fairy.

"I know," Gretta said happily. She took a tiny hand mirror out of her bag and admired herself.

"But are you nearsighted?" Morgan asked. "I didn't know you had eye trouble."

"Eye trouble?" Gretta said, surprised. Then she let out a loud peal of laughter. "Oh, Morgan, you really are a sili-ffrit. Just because a girl wears glasses, it doesn't mean she has eye trouble. They're a fashion accessory, of course."

"Oh, right. Of course," Morgan said quickly. "So tell me about Bristle. What's he like?"

"Well, he's extremely fetch, I must admit; but honestly," Gretta said, sighing, "I'm so tired of elves and wood sprites. They're so tedious. They never want to talk about anything but elf ball. And they're always upset about something."

"What do you mean?" Morgan asked.

"Well, take Bristle, for example." Gretta rummaged in her bag again. This time she pulled out a bottle of nail polish and started painting her fingernails. "Once I was just the tiniest bit late meeting him for lunch, and he was furious. It was so ridiculous."

"That is ridiculous," Morgan agreed. "Who gets upset about being a few minutes late?"

"Right. And then he kept complaining about how cold he was because the sun had gone down." Gretta frowned and shook her head.

"The sun was down?" Morgan asked. "Wait. I'm confused. I thought you said it was for lunch."

"I told you I was late," Gretta said. "Try to

pay attention here, Morgan. See, the problem was, I had this huge hag spot on my nose. Zeus, I looked like Baba Yaga! I could never have gone out looking like that. So Tuti had this great new spell for getting rid of hag spots, only it took a bit longer than we thought. So I was a little late, but only by a few hours. I mean, it wasn't like midnight or anything. And it wasn't *my* fault I had a hag spot, was it?"

"Well, everyone's late sometimes," Morgan said.

Gretta nodded. "That's exactly what I told him. And it's not as if I'm late all the time. I was on time at least once."

"So are you going to break up with him?" Morgan asked.

"I don't know. Maybe I just need a break from him." Gretta held her hand out in front of her and examined her newly painted nails. "So . . . Sam looks good. He seems a lot taller than he was."

"Yeah. He had a growth spurt last fall," Morgan said.

Gretta smiled. "I really go for tall guys, don't you?"

Morgan shrugged. "Tall is good, I guess."

"How does he like your new school?" Gretta asked.

"Sam really likes it. He's met all these techie guys. The school is full of superbrains. Sam fits right in," Morgan said sadly.

"Hmm," Gretta said, and Morgan saw that gleam in her eye, which usually meant only one thing: trouble.

"Gretta? What are you thinking?" Morgan asked.

"Oh, nothing, nothing. I just had a teensy thought, but . . . oh, never mind," Gretta said, dismissing the idea with a wave.

"Look, Gretta. I'm really, really glad you're here and all, and it's great about your book; but we have to be careful. We don't want to cause any trouble—"

Gretta held her hand up, palm out. "I completely understand, Morgan. And like I said, I have gotten so much better at my spells, I practically never screw up anymore. Anyway, I'm really just here to catch up with you and work on my book."

"That's great," Morgan said, relieved. Maybe

the fairy really had changed. "Listen, Gretta," Morgan went on, "I really should study for my English test now. It's tomorrow, and I've got to do well. This school is so hard."

"Oh, come on, Morgan," Gretta cried. "Don't be such an old glowergrim. This is my first night back. You can't study. That would be too completely boring. Hey. Want to see what Bristle looks like?"

"Sure," Morgan said. "But then I've really got to work. Do you have a picture?"

"No, but watch this. I'll need a hand mirror. Do you have one? Mine's too small."

Morgan grabbed a hand mirror from her bureau. "Like this?"

"Perfect," Gretta said. "Put it right here."

Morgan placed the mirror on the desk; and Gretta flew above it, sprinkling fairy dust from a tiny vial. Then she took her wand and tapped the mirror in several places while she muttered words. "Now, watch the mirror."

The surface of the mirror rippled and then grew cloudy. Slowly a boy came into view. He was holding a ball in one hand and seemed to be talking to someone. As Morgan watched he threw the ball and then lifted off the ground and flew.

"That's him," Gretta said. "That's Bristle. Playing elf ball as usual. I swear on my crown, that's all he ever does."

"He is cute, though." Morgan clapped her hands. "Gretta, this is amazing!"

The image in the mirror grew blurry, and Bristle was gone.

"Wow. That is so cool," Morgan said.

"See," Gretta said proudly. "I told you I've gotten better."

"You have. I'm impressed," Morgan told her. "But now I've really got to study. Maybe you could work on your book." Morgan opened her English text to the section called "Introduction to the Romantic Poets."

"There's plenty of time for that later," Gretta told her. "Right now I'm going to check out your closet and see what new clothes you've gotten."

Morgan tried to concentrate on her work while Gretta flew off to the closet.

"These red platforms are fabulous!" Gretta called. "What do you wear them with? You've got to try them on for me."

An hour later Gretta and Morgan were talking about whether her black tank top looked better with her new jeans or her red skirt, when Sally knocked on her door and asked, "Morgan, is Sam in there?"

"No, Sally. He's up in his room, I think," Morgan called.

"That's good because it's past ten and you two should turn in," Sally told her. "I thought I heard you talking to someone."

"Oh, I was, uh, reading my history paper over. It helps to read it out loud before you revise." Morgan went to the door and gave Sally a hug. "'Night, Sally."

As soon as Sally left, Morgan whispered, "Gretta! What am I going to do? It's time for bed, and I haven't studied one bit!"

"Not a problem!" Gretta told her. "Remember the Knowledge Enhancement Spell I put on you in September? It worked great, didn't it?"

Morgan frowned. "I couldn't sleep with the book under my pillow. I took it out after half an hour. It didn't do a thing."

"You passed the test, though, right?" Gretta asked.

"Just barely. And it had nothing to do with the spell."

"Ha. That's what you think," Gretta told her. "That half hour probably helped enough to at least let you pass. Think what might have happened without it. Wait right here." The fairy flew to the dollhouse and disappeared inside for a minute. She reappeared with her *Introduction to the Fairy Arts* textbook and sat on the dollhouse steps, flipping through it. "Here we go!" she said. "KES number six."

"What is KES again?" Morgan asked.

"Knowledge Enhancement Spell," Gretta explained. " 'Place relevant text under subject's pillow at bedtime. Repeat the following incantation while passing wand over subject's head. For best results subject should sleep at least six hours.' "

"I don't know, Gretta," Morgan said, remembering all the disasters from Gretta's earlier visit.

"Morgan, I've learned a lot since the last time I was here. And the KES are the easiest kinds of spells."

"But—"

"Trust me. This spell is totally gnome-proof," Gretta insisted.

"That's what you said about the one that turned me bright blue."

"But that was ages ago. I didn't know anything then compared to what I know now. You just hop into bed and leave the rest to me."

From the Journal of Gretta Fleetwing

Well, here I am back at Morgan's—actually not *back* at Morgan's because they have moved to a new castle—but I am staying with Morgan once again, offering my help and guidance as she makes (well, *tries* to make—she so seriously needs my help!) the adjustment to her new school (if one can call it a school; I personally call it a troll hole. Honestly, these human schools are not fit for . . . well, more on that subject later).

Poor Morgan! It's really quite touching to see how much she missed me. When she heard my laughter and knew I was back, she was so happy her crown lit up!

We played an amusing little trick on her stepbrother, Sam, involving his robot, Marvin. It was quite hilarious, and I'm glad to see that in spite of her trials, Morgan has not lost her sense of humor. Oh, we will have fun this visit!

I did have to explain to Morgan that I have serious and

important work to do and will not be able to fly to her every time she flaps her wings. I must be firm with her on this matter. She has already insisted that I tell her all about Bristle and even begged me to conjure up his image in a mirror so she could see what he looks like.

Naturally she was amazed by my conjuring skills, and absolutely crushing on Bristle when she saw him. Zeus, I think she would have jumped right into the mirror after him if I hadn't restrained her. Well, Bristle *is* fetch, but as I have tried to teach Morgan, looks aren't everything (don't get me wrong—you'll never see Gretta dating a ballybog—there are limits!); and one must take other considerations into account when choosing a mate, like maybe someone who can converse on a subject other than elf ball! And maybe someone who understands that busy fairies might be a *teensy* bit late now and then. Grrr! Every time I think of the way Bristle tries to control me, it just makes my crown spin. Morgan agrees that he was being completely unreasonable, and she thinks Tuti is right that a little time away from him will make him realize that I am not the kind of girlfriend who will allow herself to be taken for granted.

So here I am!

I told Morgan all about my book, and she offered to help me with my research. I explained to her that a serious scholar should not be expected to conform to pointless rules and regulations, a concept that the Elder Fairies cannot seem to grasp. It is incomprehensible that they have suspended me when all I was trying to do was complete my assignments in a timely manner. Is it *my* fault that my wand malfunctioned? I certainly didn't *intend* to set Professor Thornly's robe on fire. Of course I can't blame him for being upset. If my knees looked like his, I would definitely not want them exposed!

Perhaps I wasn't entirely honest with Morgan about the reason for my visit. I may have forgotten to mention my suspension, but it's hard enough to convince her that occasionally spells are necessary. I don't want her to doubt my abilities, which, if I may say, have greatly improved since the last time I was here! Well, she'll find out tomorrow when the KES works its magic.

Yes, I have had to rescue the sili-ffrit already! She was so excited to see me she was flying in circles, and she insisted on showing me every item in her closet, forgetting all about the English test she was supposed to study for. So of course it's Gretta to the rescue once again! What's a fairy to do?

I must admit it is nice to be back in the dollhouse. Morgan's new room is really something. And now that Sam lives here in the same castle, well, the possibilities are endless.

For research I mean.

Coming here was absolutely the right decision. Morgan definitely needs my help, poor trowling. She has made no friends and obviously is not adjusting well. I must make her understand that if she is to make friends she needs to stop being so self-conscious and self-absorbed. Honestly, these humans think about nothing except their image. They are so caught up in frivolous materialism. Well, fortunately Gretta is here to guide and advise her.

And now I really must turn in. A fairy needs her beauty sleep, and all this scholarly work really has my wings sagging. Yawn!

And so to bed. Oh, I almost forgot. I have to call Tuti! I can't possibly go to sleep without getting the Bristle report!

Chapter Two

Sam was eating his cereal and reading *Science News* the next morning when Morgan came into the kitchen. "Morning, Sam," she said. At least that's what she meant to say. It came out, " 'Hail to thee, blithe Spirit!' "

"Huh?" Sam said.

"Percy Bysshe Shelley, 1820."

"Still studying?" Sam asked without looking up from his magazine.

" 'Souls of Poets dead and gone,' " Morgan said. What was this? Why was she quoting poetry?

"I know. The Romantic poets. Who cares?" Sam said.

"John Keats, 1818."

"Yeah, well, I'm trying to read, Morg. Do you have to recite the poems?"

" 'Scorn not the Sonnet'—"

"Knock it off, Morgan," Sam grumbled.

"William Wordsworth, 1827." Morgan clapped her hand over her mouth. *Gretta!* The KES spell.

Sam took his cereal bowl to the sink. "Look, I gotta get there early today. Are you ready, or should I go without you?"

" 'Fare thee well! And if for ever—Still for ever, fare *thee well*'!" Morgan said, waving at him.

"Whatever," Sam said. He grabbed his backpack and left.

Morgan raced upstairs and pounded on the dollhouse. " 'Up! up! my Friend, and clear your looks; Why all this toil and trouble?' " she shouted.

She kept pounding until she heard Gretta grumbling sleepily. "Zeus and Apollo. What's going on?"

"Wordsworth, 1798."

In a minute Gretta stumbled to the door, rubbing her eyes. She was wearing an oversized T-shirt and boxers, and her hair was a mess. "Morgan? What's up?"

"'A spirit seizes me and speaks within'!" Morgan shouted.

Gretta frowned. "Morgan, I came here to get a break, and I would really—"

Morgan slapped her forehead. "'But mine own words, I pray, deny me not'! Percy Bysshe Shelley, 1819!" She ran to her bed and pulled her English text from under her pillow. "'What was that curse? For ye all heard me speak'!!!" She shook the book and pointed at Gretta.

Gretta yawned. "If you wanted someone to help you study, you should have asked Sam because—"

Morgan stamped her foot and slammed the book down on her desk. How could she make Gretta understand? She grabbed a piece of paper and a pencil, praying the writing would not come out as poetry. She wrote, "I can only speak poems. Do something!" She held the paper down for Gretta to read.

"Oh I get it. You're spouting," Gretta told her, giggling.

"'Speak the words which I would hear'!"

"Just take it easy, Morgan. Spouting is a very common problem with KES spells."

"'It tears me as fire tears a thundercloud'!"

"Just hang on a sec." Gretta disappeared inside and came back with her IFA text and began flipping through it.

"'Who dares? For I would hear that curse again. Ha, what an awful whisper rises up!'" Morgan sank down onto the carpet and sat with her head in her hands. How could she have been stupid enough to let Gretta do this to her? What had she been thinking? Well, she'd been desperate. She needed a good grade on this test.

Gretta flipped through her IFA, muttering, "Spouting, reversal, hmm, let's see—"

"'Misery, O misery to me,'" Morgan said, sighing.

"I think I better give Tuti a call. She's really good at this stuff." Gretta whipped out her cell phone and dialed.

"Tuti, hey." She chatted away for a few minutes. "Are you kidding? Really? That's unbelievable. What trolls!"

Morgan sank even lower. Maybe she just wouldn't go to school today. So what if she missed the English test. If only she could go back to her old school.

Gretta looked over at Morgan. "Zeus, girl, it's not the end of the world. I'll fix it."

Morgan shrugged.

Gretta spoke into the phone again. "Look, Tuti. We have a tiny bit of a problem here. Morgan's spouting, and she's not too happy about it."

Gretta listened for a minute. "Uh-huh, uh-huh. Well, that sounds easy enough . . . oh. Really? That's a great idea!" She glanced at Morgan. "Yes, she could definitely use a little of that. Thanks, Tute. You're the best. I'll call you after I've dealt here." Gretta hung up and turned to Morgan. "Okay. Let's get started." She rummaged in her bag and pulled out several little vials. Then she flipped through her spell textbook. "This is so simple!" she said, and drew a circle on the rug. "Okay. Kneel inside the circle, Morgan," Gretta commanded. Morgan knelt.

Gretta flew in front of her and put three drops of a tincture on Morgan's forehead. Then she flew around her, waving her wand and muttering words. Finally she sprinkled some fairy dust over her. "Okay, Morgan. That's it. Stand up and say something."

Morgan stood up. "This better have wor—I can talk! No more poems! Thank heavens!"

"No. Thank Gretta," the fairy said proudly.

"Except that if it wasn't for you, I wouldn't have been speaking in poems to begin with," Morgan reminded her.

As she walked to school, Morgan felt curiously happy. Strangely she almost felt like skipping. It might be weird to skip, but so what? She could skip if she felt like it. As she skipped along she decided that her school wasn't so bad. In fact, it was kind of fun. She really, really liked school.

"Hello there!" Morgan called when she passed a group of kids. She didn't know them, but that was no reason not to say hello to them. They stared at her; and one of them nodded and mumbled, "S'up."

The test was pretty hard, and Morgan didn't know most of the answers; but she did her best and was sure it would be fine. She wasn't one bit worried.

At lunch Sam asked how it went.

"Oh I don't know. I didn't know most of the

answers. Anyway, who cares? It's just an English test," Morgan said with a laugh. "Come on. Let's go sit with your Tech Club friends."

Since they had both started in the second semester, and neither of them knew any kids, Morgan and Sam had eaten lunch together the first few weeks they had been at the new school. Now that Sam had made some friends in the Tech Club, he usually ate with them, and Morgan ate with a couple of kids from her homeroom.

Sam looked surprised. "But I thought you didn't like the Tech Club kids. You said they were brainiacs."

Morgan laughed. "Oh Sam. Of course I like them."

"But you said they don't talk about anything but computers, and you don't understand half of what they say."

"Well, I can learn, can't I?"

Sam shrugged, and they went to the table where he usually sat. "You guys know Morgan, don't you?"

"Hi, everyone!" Morgan said loudly.

They nodded at her. "Hey, Morgan," Sam's friend James said.

Morgan put her tray next to Sam's and sat down. "Wow. This looks really good."

"Yeah. I just love good old mystery meat. Just don't drop it. It'll probably bounce," James said.

Morgan laughed. "No, but it really is delicious," she said, taking a big bite.

James was sitting across from Morgan. He looked at Sam. "Is she for real?"

"Well, there's just no point in dwelling on the negatives. You've got to be positive!" Morgan chirped.

Sam laughed. "Great imitation, Morg. You sound exactly like your dad."

A girl named Marissa nodded. "I get it. My mom is always saying stuff like that. Like, 'Oh Marissa, can't you ever look on the bright side?'"

James laughed, too. "Yeah," he said, spearing his meat. "Too bad the only sides of this are burned and more burned."

"So how's the game coming?" another guy asked Sam, and they all began talking about the video games they were working on.

"Wow. That is so cool. I can't believe you guys know how to do all that stuff," Morgan said.

James smiled. Then he shrugged and said, "It's not really that hard. Once you learn some programming, it's pretty easy."

"Sam's Iditarod game is amazing. Tell me about your game," Morgan said, and James spent the rest of the lunch period explaining his game to her in minute detail.

They finished lunch; and as they were busing their trays, Sam whispered, "Sorry about that."

"Sorry? What do you mean?" Morgan asked.

Sam looked surprised. "I just thought you might be really bored. I mean, once James starts talking about his game, he tends to go on and on."

"Oh, but I thought it was fascinating, Sam."

"Y-you did?"

"Yes. And James is so nice. In fact they're all nice. I'm really glad I'm getting to know them better."

Sam stared at her. "Are you okay?" he asked.

"Of course I'm okay, Sam. Why wouldn't I be?"

"You're acting kind of weird," Sam said.

"I am? Weird how?" she asked.

"I don't know. Just all, like, happy or something."

Morgan laughed loudly. "Oh Sam. You're

funny." She was headed to her history classroom when James came up to her and said, "Hey, Morgan. If you want I could bring my game in tomorrow and show you how it works."

"Wow. That'd be cool, James," Morgan said.

"Okay. See you tomorrow, then."

"Great." As James and Sam went on down the hall, Morgan heard James say, "Dude, your sister's cool."

All through Morgan's three afternoon classes, she felt great. She even raised her hand a few times, something she was usually too shy to do since she had moved to this school. She got a couple answers right, but in math she messed up. "Oops. Guess I blew that one," she blurted out.

Some of the kids around her laughed, and even her teacher chuckled sympathetically. "It's perfectly all right to make mistakes, Morgan. If we never made mistakes, we wouldn't learn much, would we?" he said.

"Let's hope he remembers that next time he's grading our tests," the guy behind her whispered.

Morgan turned around and gave him a big smile.

As she was going to her locker at the end of the day, she saw a notice about a meeting for kids who wanted to join the newspaper. Her parents kept telling her she needed to get involved in some activities. They were right, she decided. She would go to the meeting. She would get involved. It would be a great way to get to know some people.

She went to the classroom where the meeting was to take place. The room was pretty full, and Morgan took one of the last open desks. Soon after she sat down, a ninth-grade girl stood up and said, "Hi, everyone. Welcome to the Culver Junior High *Banner.* I'm so glad to see such a great turnout. Putting out this newspaper is a lot of work, and we really need help. I'm going to tell you what we do, and how you can help."

Morgan thought it sounded like fun; and when the meeting was over she went up to the editor and said, "It sounds really interesting. I'd like to sign up."

"Great," the editor said. "Put your name and number here, and we'll call you. Have you ever worked on a paper before?"

"I haven't," Morgan said. "But I've always done

pretty well in English. And I'd love to learn about writing articles."

"Terrific. That's a great attitude!" the editor said. "See you at the next meeting."

"Okay. Thanks!" Morgan called happily as she headed for the door. If she hurried she could make it to the Green Team meeting. They did recycling, gardening, and other kinds of environmental work; and Morgan definitely wanted to help out.

From the Journal of Gretta Fleetwing

It must have been my fairy intuition at work, telling me how serious Morgan's situation was (is?). Whichever. The poor girl is an emotional wreck! I got here just in time and not a moment too soon. If ever there was a human in need of fairy assistance, it is her (she?). Whatever. I don't care what Madame Featherwright says: these grammatical trifles will be dealt with by my editor. Which reminds me, I wonder how much gold they will give me for my advance. I do hope it's a lot!

This morning I was finally getting some much-needed sleep when I was awakened by the most horrible racket. I truly thought there was a herd of unicorns stampeding on my roof! My entire castle was shaking! My ears are still ringing from the noise. Of course I leaped immediately from my bed, thinking something truly disastrous had occurred, only to find that Morgan, apparently suffering a break with reality, had mistaken my roof for an acorn drum! I'm telling you, a fanggen could not have made half the noise she made up there.

I have to say that I'm not at all surprised that Morgan is having trouble fitting into her new school. If she over-reacts to everything the way she overreacted to a simple case of spouting, which any fairy will tell you is *very* common and almost unavoidable with KES, it's really no wonder. Of course I quickly sorted it all out and was able to reverse the spell without much trouble.

I finally got Morgan calmed down and shooed her off to school, which, I have reason to believe, she will find quite enjoyable. Morgan doesn't know this, but I sprinkled a teensy bit of happy powder over her when I reversed her spouting. It was Tuti's idea—and a truly brilliant one I have to say.

After Morgan left I tried to get some work done; but what with the nerve-shattering start to my day, I found I couldn't concentrate. I went back to bed and slept all morning and part of the afternoon, which just shows you how emotionally drained I am!

Now back to the books!

Hmm. I wonder when Morgan will be home. Soon I hope. It is a bit lonely here all by myself. There's no one home but me and Hattie, Morgan's funny old dog. She stays outside all day except when Morgan's here. I can see her from Morgan's window out in the yard, chasing birds. What a sili-ffrit she is. Not the sharpest quill on the porcupine, but she's really very cute. I do wish she wasn't quite so big. Oh dear. Watching Hattie makes me miss Oliver, my pet lightning bug. Maybe I should have brought him after all; but last time he was so disobedient, and he was always getting lost. One more distraction that I don't need. But still, he is such good company.

Where did I put my cell phone, I wonder? Oh. Here it is. I better check my messages. Hmm. Nothing from Bristle. I did tell him not to call, but he might at least have wanted to make sure I'm still alive. He's probably too busy playing elf ball. Zeus forbid he should have to think about me for even the two seconds it would take him to send me a text message.

I wonder if boy humans are as inconsiderate as elves. (Note to self: Important! Research boy humans. How do they compare to elves? wood sprites?) Oh! I just had a brilliant idea. I'll begin my boy-human research in Sam's room. What could be better? I'll just fly up to his room and have a look around.

* * *

Well, Sammy's room was full of revelations! I had no idea that boy humans are so much more exciting than elves. Sammy has the cutest photos on his desk. There's the dearest one of him and Morgan when they were little trowlings. How sweet is that? And one of him on a boat with an older man—his papa maybe? That one is particularly interesting because Sammy is wearing only a bathing suit and oh-la-la, he really is quite buff! I would love to know more about his workout routine and see a demonstration, perhaps—strictly for research purposes, of course. One thing I'm sure of: It involves more than playing elf ball 24/7.

Sammy also has a truly crown-lifting computer with lots of extra parts attached to it. I'm sure he does brilliant work on it. I accidentally sat on one of the keys, and it made kind of a loud noise—a whirre-clickity-clickity-whirre sort of noise. It scared me so much I almost lost my wand! I'm pretty sure I didn't disturb anything; but even if I did, I know I can fix it with a simple reversing spell.

I would have stayed up there much longer; but I think Morgan will be home soon, and I'm not sure she would approve of me being in his room. She has some silly ideas about privacy and doesn't believe in what she calls "snooping" and I call researching. Of course Morgan doesn't understand the importance of my work.

Which reminds me, I really must talk to her about my

castle. She's let it fall into a sad state of disrepair. I love Morgan dearly, but honestly humans can be so inconsiderate sometimes! She needs to understand that if she plans to accommodate guests, she has got to keep the place up.

Note to self: Tell Morgan she *must* get following items:

1. New bedsheets—old ones horrible and scratchy.
2. New pillow—must be milkweed down; I'm allergic to all others.
3. New mirror for bathroom—old one impossibly blurry.
4. Wide-screen TV—Tuti says iPod video player best model.

Chapter Three

By the time Morgan got home, it was almost six o'clock, and Gretta was sitting on the steps of the dollhouse, waiting for her.

"Where've you been?" Gretta asked when she saw Morgan. "I've been waiting for you for hours."

"At school, of course. Where else?"

"All this time? Zeus, that place really is a dungeon. No wonder you can't stand it."

"Well, actually, today wasn't that bad."

"Oh really? How did the test go?"

"Okay, I think. I don't really know."

"So what else happened?"

"I signed up to work on the newspaper. And I joined the Green Team."

"Really? The newspaper?"

"Uh-huh."

"Oh. Well, that's great. Except those newspaper people can be *sooo* boring. And they take themselves *so* seriously! Honestly the elves at the *Fairy Post Gazette*—" Gretta's phone rang. "Hold on a minute, Morgan. That's Tuti," she said, flipping open her phone.

Morgan sat down at her desk and pulled her books out of her backpack. She was about to start her homework when she heard Gretta say, "You know, I think it did. She joined some clubs and seems happier. Of course, who knows what happens tomorrow when it's worn off."

When it's worn off? What was Gretta talking about?

Morgan tried to hear more, but Gretta was whispering.

As soon as Gretta hung up, Morgan said, "Gretta, I heard you talking to Tuti. What did you mean 'when it's worn off'?"

"I—I don't know what you're talking about, Morgan. You must have misheard me."

"Gretta, I know what I heard. What kind of spell did you put on me?"

"I took off the spouting, just like you asked me to."

"And?"

Gretta giggled. "Well, I did mix the teeniest bit of happy dust in with the reversal powder."

"Happy dust?" Morgan shouted.

"It was Tuti's idea," Gretta said quickly.

"I don't care if it was Albert Einstein's idea. You can't just go around putting spells on people."

"Oh Morgan, get over it. You seemed so down. I just wanted to give you a lift, that's all."

"I cannot believe you did that. You know I don't like spells. Especially when you mess them up all the time."

"Well, it worked this time, didn't it? I told you I've gotten better. And look. You joined some clubs. You met some new people. Where's the harm?"

"The harm is that I just want to be myself, not some perky Pollyanna."

"Polly who?"

"Pollyan—oh never mind." Morgan put her hands to her head. "They probably all think I'm some cheery freaky weirdo, thanks to you and your happy powder."

"Well, excuse me for trying to cheer you up a bit." Gretta went back inside the dollhouse, slamming the door behind her. "Some thanks I get. Remind me never to try to help you out again."

But that night at dinner, when Morgan told her family that she had joined the newspaper and the environmental club, they were thrilled. Her father said, "That's wonderful, honey. See, I knew you would find a place at that school. It just takes time. And a positive attitude."

Sam looked at Morgan, and they both started to laugh.

"What's so funny?" her dad asked.

"Nothing, Dad. Just something that happened at lunch."

Maybe Gretta's happy powder hadn't really hurt anything. In fact, maybe it had even helped a bit, Morgan admitted. She fixed Gretta a little plate of food and took it up to her room.

She knelt beside the dollhouse and knocked on the door. "Gretta, I'm sorry about what I said earlier, about how you mess up your spells."

"Humph!"

"I've got some dinner for you. It's really good tonight."

The door of the dollhouse opened, and Gretta appeared. She took the plate from Morgan and sat down on the steps.

"Look, Gretta, I know you meant well with the happy powder. And you're right. You have gotten much better. But no more spells. Okay?"

"Okay, okay. I was only trying to help," Gretta said, digging into her dinner.

"I know," Morgan said. "Okay. Now I've really got to work on my science homework, so when you finish eating why don't you work on your book? How's it going, anyway?"

"It's going beautifully," Gretta told her. "But there are a few things I need to talk to you about, Morgan." She put down her plate and opened her journal and read Morgan the list of things she needed.

"An iPod?" Morgan cried. "Gretta, do you know how much those things cost? Believe me, I'd love to have a video iPod, but if I get one I'm not leaving it in the dollhouse."

"Oh. Well, I assumed you wanted me to be comfortable, but I see I was wrong," Gretta said.

"Gretta, of course I want you to be comfortable," Morgan told her. "But I just can't afford to buy you an iPod. Anyway, you're a fairy. Why don't you just conjure one up?"

Gretta sighed. "Morgan, you just got through telling me no more spells. Could we be a teensy bit more consistent here?" Gretta took out her pen. "Anyway, you know the Elder Fairies would have a fit if I started conjuring up iPods." She turned to a new page in her journal and began to write. "Although I'm sure I could do it, if I wanted to," she added.

"I'm sure you could, too, but you're right. No more spells," Morgan told her. "I can't get you an iPod, but I will make you some new sheets and a quilt."

"Well, that's a start, I guess," Gretta grumbled.

Morgan went to her desk and took out her science book. She struggled with it for a few minutes and finally said, "I don't get this homework. I'm going to ask Sam about this."

"I'll come with you," Gretta said.

"You will?" Morgan said, doubtfully.

"Sure. He won't be able to see me, of course, but I have to observe him for my research."

"Right, well, okay, but don't get any ideas about spells," Morgan warned.

"No spells. I swear on my crown."

Gretta hopped onto Morgan's shoulder, and they went up to Sam's room, where the fairy settled herself on the edge of Sam's desk. She took out her notebook and began taking notes, looking so serious it was all Morgan could do to keep from laughing.

Sam showed Morgan how to do the science homework; and then he said, "Hey, want to see something cool? Look at this new section of my game. I finished it last night." He fiddled with his computer for a minute and then frowned. "What . . . ? This is weird."

"What's wrong?" Morgan asked.

"My game. The whole third level is missing!"

"Missing?"

"Like it's been deleted or something."

"That's impossible, Sam. No one would come in here and mess with your computer. Everyone knows better than to touch it."

Sam was fiddling frantically, clicking keys and bringing up windows. "I don't believe this. Do you know how long it will take to reconstruct that section? And the contest is next week."

"Did you back it up?" Morgan asked.

"I think I have part of it backed up, but the disk is at school. I'm going to have to spend the whole weekend working on this. I don't see how this happened."

"Poor Sammy," Gretta said when they had gone downstairs.

"I know. But he'll get it back. He always over-reacts when it comes to his game." Morgan started reading her notes, hoping Gretta would take the hint and let her get back to work.

"You know, Morgan, I've been thinking," Gretta announced.

Morgan looked up at her. "Uh-oh."

"What?" the fairy asked innocently.

Morgan smiled. "Call me crazy, but the thought of you thinking scares me a bit."

"Oh, you old glowergrim." Gretta laughed. "Actually, though, maybe I'll just surprise you."

"Why does that not make me feel any better?" Morgan asked.

"Don't worry," Gretta assured her. "You'll love it. Trust me."

From the Journal of Gretta Fleetwing

Even though Morgan did not appreciate my help, it's clear that giving her the happy powder was the right thing to do. She came home last evening with a much better attitude about her new school, and she has even joined some organizations. She's going to be working for the newspaper, and she's joined a group called the Green Team, which is some sort of cycling team. Sounds pretty dull, but I guess going biking is better than sitting around moping. And I'm sure she will look very cute in her cycling outfit. I wonder if she'll have to wear one of those strange-looking hats I've seen humans wearing when they ride their bicycles. I do hope not.

One thing I'm learning is that most humans think they are a lot smarter than they are. For example last night Morgan and Sam were talking about their homework for something called physics, which had to do with this guy named Al Einstein, who is supposed to be this supergenius. The reason they think he's so smart is that he came up with this theory about his relatives, which basically says that they have a lot of mass and not much energy. Well, hel-lo. Anyone who's ever met my Aunt Pollonia and Uncle Gumquat could have told them that!

Ah well, no one ever said the life of a scholar would be

easy, and I try to remember that having a challenging human like Morgan to cope with is all to the good as far as my research and my book are concerned. Of course the Elder Fairies are so absolutely clueless about humans that they probably wouldn't know it if one landed on their shoulder, er, I mean, if the fairy landed on a human's shoulder. Even the Elder Fairies, clueless as they are, would notice if a human landed on their shoulder. Ha-ha!

But be that as it may, I take heart in knowing that fairykind will benefit from the trials and tribulations I am currently undergoing. And now that the castle is quiet, I think a nap is in order. More later.

Oops, I overslept a bit. I must hurry because I have to help Sammy with something before they get home. Apparently he lost part of the computer game he's been working on for some contest, and the poor boy was devastated. I did wonder if I might possibly have caused the glitch when I sat on the keys, but I'm sure that had nothing to do with it. Everyone knows how unreliable computers are.

But anyway, I will sprinkle some Restore drops on the keys, and that should take care of the problem. How surprised he'll be when he turns his computer on tonight and finds the game good as new.

Now just let me find my spell bag. Here it is, and off I go.

Sammy's room really is so fascinating. I just love looking at his things. I could spend hours—oh dear—is that Morgan I hear? Zeus. I've got to do this fast and get out of here before she catches me. Fortunately it's a simple task. A few sprays—one more for good measure—and there we go. Good as new, no doubt!

Chapter Four

When Morgan and Sam got home from school, Sally said, "Listen, kids, I've invited our neighbors Mr. and Mrs. Saunders over for dinner tonight, so get cleaned up, and best behavior, please."

"Who are they?" Sam asked.

"They live in that big house on the corner. Mrs. Saunders is on practically every charity board in town, so they entertain all the time. She'd be a great client for my catering business, so I want dinner to be exceptionally impressive."

"Exceptionally boring, you mean," Sam mumbled.

"Don't start, Sam," Sally snapped. She was up to her elbows in pastry dough. "They seem like very nice people. And their grandson goes to Culver. He's in ninth grade, I believe."

"*Duncan* Saunders?" Morgan asked.

"Yes, I think she did say his name was Duncan," Sally said. "Do you know him, Morgan?"

"Not really, but I've seen him around," Morgan said. He had smiled at her a few times, one of the few people who had; and Morgan thought he was hot. She had asked Marcie Denton, a girl in her English class who knew everyone, who he was.

Morgan went up to her room to change out of her jeans and into a skirt and a sweater. Gretta was sitting on the doorstep of the dollhouse, talking on her cell phone as usual. "He said that?" Morgan heard her say. "So he really misses me, huh? Well, serves him right. What a boggle-bo!"

Gretta finished her call and stood up, snapping her cell phone shut.

"What was that all about?" Morgan asked.

"Well, apparently Bristle's been wondering where I've gone," Gretta told her. "He's trying to get Tuti to tell him so he can come and get me.

Ha! As if I'll go home just because he wants me to. Besides, I've got work to do here."

"It's kind of sweet that he misses you, though, don't you think?" Morgan said.

"No!" Gretta stamped her foot. "He's just being his dwergish, possessive self. He thinks he owns me. He has a hag fit if I even look at another guy."

Morgan felt a twinge of pity for Bristle. Being Gretta's boyfriend would not be easy. She didn't say anything to Gretta, though.

"So why the skirt? Are we going out somewhere?" Gretta asked.

"No. The Saunders are coming for dinner." Morgan told her what Sally had said.

"Hmm. Sounds like a snooze cruise. Count me out."

"At least the food will be good. Sally's going all out. I'll bring you some when we're done."

"Yum!" Gretta said, patting her stomach.

Morgan was just about to go see if she could help Sally when Sam banged downstairs and burst into her room.

"Morgy!" He spread his arms wide and gave

Morgan a bear hug, and then pushed her away. "Wanna hear a funny song, Morgy? 'Greasy gimey goppor's guts, mootilated monkeys' . . . *Ha! Ha!* I can't 'member! You 'member, Morgy?"

"S-Sam? Wh-what's up?" Morgan asked. She looked at Gretta and whispered, "What have you done to him?"

Sam frowned, screwing up his whole face and peering at Morgan. "Whadda matter, Morgy? You hungry? Me hungry. Sammy hungry, Morgy. You got candy, Morgy?

"Watch this, Morgy. I can do somersaults," he said, flinging himself on the floor of Morgan's room.

Gretta was rummaging in her spell bag. She pulled out a tiny glass bottle and said, "Uh-oh."

"What?" Morgan demanded.

"It's not a big problem, Morgan. It's just, well, I was pretty angry when I was packing to come here. I thought I grabbed the Restore drops, but I must have grabbed my mom's Rejuvi drops instead." Gretta laughed. "They help you feel ten years younger, which is a good thing for a 4,032-year-old fairy. But I guess it's not so great for a fourteen-year-old boy human."

"So Sam feels like a four-year-old?"

"Look, Morgy. I can bounce," Sam shouted. He had jumped onto Morgan's bed and was bouncing as if it were a trampoline. "Come on! It's fun!"

Gretta nodded. "Just relax, Morgan. This is not a big problem. It's easy to fix." She was flipping through her textbook when the phone rang. "It's Tuti. Just let me get this."

Gretta explained the problem to Tuti, and then said, "Uh-huh. Right. Right. That sounds simple enough."

Sam kept on bouncing and singing.

Then Morgan heard Gretta say, "Hmm. That could be a slight problem. Well, they probably don't have any just lying around. Hold on. I'll ask."

Gretta looked at Morgan. "You wouldn't happen to have any pigs' bladders lying around, would you?"

"*What?*"

"Pigs' bladders. See, tincture of pigs' bladders is a neutralizing agent. We fairies always keep a few pigs' bladders handy for emergencies, but I guess humans don't, do they?"

Morgan rolled her eyes. She was trying to keep Sam from wrecking her room.

"Well, without pigs' bladders we're kind of stuck temporarily." She spoke into the phone again. "Would you? Fantastic! Thanks, Tuti. See you in a few."

"Tuti's going to get some tincture, and I'll go meet her. Then we'll do the reversal. So just sit tight. I'll be back in a jiff."

Gretta flew off, and Morgan said, "Sam, listen. We have to be quiet because your mom is getting ready for her guests."

Sam kept on jumping. "Guests, guests, silly, stupid guests," he sang. "Who wants to meet some silly, stupid guests? Not me, not me, not me. Not going to meet some silly, stupid guests."

"Shhh, Sam. You've got to be quiet."

"Don't have to be quiet. You're not my mother. You're just a creepy girl."

"Sam, let's play a game, okay?"

Sam stopped bouncing. "What game?"

"Umm. Come sit down here on the floor, and I'll show you. It's really fun."

Sam jumped off the bed and sat down on the floor. "Okay. What's the game, Morgy?"

Morgan thought hard. What kind of game could they play that would keep him quiet?

"Umm, it's a pretend game, Sam. First let's pretend we're asleep. So you have to be really quiet." Morgan lay down on her side and pretended to snore softly. Sam did the same; but in two seconds he said, "Don't like this game. Wanna be a gorilla." He jumped up and started scratching his sides and making gorilla noises.

"Okay, forget pretending." Morgan grabbed a deck of cards. "How about cards, Sam? You like cards, right?"

"Ooo-ooo-ooo-oooh. Gorillas don't like cards."

Morgan rummaged in her backpack and found a half-eaten bag of M&M's. "Look, Sam. Look what I have."

"Candy?"

"M&M's. You love these."

"I have some, Morgy?" Sam asked, holding out his hand.

"You can have some, but you have to win them. We'll play cards for them. Okay?"

Sam sat down, and they played cards until Gretta finally appeared.

"It's about time," Morgan whispered. "I'm almost out of M&M's. Did you get it?"

"Yes. And let me tell you, it wasn't easy. I had to go all the way to—"

"Whatever, Gretta—just do it. Quick, before he starts jumping around again."

Sam was lying on his back on the floor, playing with Hattie.

Gretta splashed a few drops of the tincture of pigs' bladders over his head, said an incantation, and waved her wand. "Okay. That should do it."

"That's it?" Morgan asked.

Sam sat up, blinking his eyes. "Man. I must have fallen asleep. I just had the weirdest dream."

"Yeah. You fell asleep for a few minutes. And now you've got to get out of here. Sally's guests will be here in a few minutes, and I've got to get changed."

After Sam went back to his room, Morgan changed quickly and went downstairs to help Sally.

"Everything smells great," Morgan told her.

"Let's hope it tastes great, too," Sally said.

They finished setting the table just as the

Saunders arrived. Mr. Saunders was a pleasant-looking man, with a reddish face, thick white eyebrows, and a fringe of white hair around his otherwise bald head. Mrs. Saunders was tall and slender. Her black hair was streaked with gray and pulled back into an elegant chignon. They smiled as they shook hands with Morgan and Sam.

"What lovely children," Mrs. Saunders said to Sally. "And what delicious smells are coming from the kitchen. Everyone simply raves about your cooking, my dear. We're thrilled to get a taste of it."

Morgan was nervous as she and Sam helped Sally carry the plates in and out of the kitchen. She knew this meant a lot to Sally. But when they were about halfway through the meal, she started to relax. The food was delicious, and the Saunders seemed to love everything they tasted. Mrs. Saunders turned to Morgan and asked, "And how are you liking Culver, my dear? Our grandson, Duncan, is in the ninth grade there."

Morgan nodded. "It's okay. At first I missed my old school a lot, but now I'm getting used to Culver."

"And what about you, Sam?" she asked.

"I like it. They've got a great *snort oink snort*—" he clapped a hand over his mouth.

"Good heavens, Sam. Did something go down the wrong way?" Sally asked.

Sam blushed and stammered, "Excuse me."

"Are you all right, son?" Morgan's father asked.

"Yeah," Sam said, his face still bright red. "I'm okay. I just *oioink oioink snort.*"

Mr. Saunders looked at him with interest. "I myself suffer occasionally from a similar malady, my boy. My wife blames it on my tendency to overeat; but as I've tried to explain to her, it is probably caused by allergies—"

"*Oioink oioink snort,*" went Sam.

Morgan, her dad, Sally, and the Saunders were all staring at him openmouthed.

"Sam, this is *not* amusing," Sally said. "The dinner table is not—"

"I'm really sor—*oinkk oink snort.*"

"You see, my dear, I told you my condition is quite common. This healthy young man suffers even more than—"

"*Snoort snoorrt oinkk.* I'm sorry," Sam said, and he jumped up. "I need to be *snort oioink*

excused." He grabbed his plate, rushed into the kitchen with it, and then raced upstairs.

"Oh dear," Sally said. "I'd better go make sure he's okay." She started to get up, but Morgan jumped up first. "I'll go, Sally. You stay with your guests. I'll call you if he gets any worse."

Morgan rushed up to her room. "Gretta! What have you done to Sam?" she cried, pounding on the dollhouse.

"Now what?" Gretta asked, sounding very annoyed. "Honestly I don't see how I'm supposed to get anything done when you are constantly banging on my roof like some kind of bubak."

"Come on. We've got to help Sam. He's making these weird pig noises. Snorting and oinking."

"Hmm," Gretta said, hopping onto Morgan's shoulder. "Sounds like he's got the snorts. It's nothing to worry about, Morgan."

"Nothing to worry about? Are you crazy?" As they raced upstairs they heard Sam, "*Snort snort oink oink snort.*"

Gretta laughed. "Zeus, sounds like he's got one serious case."

"Sam? Are you okay?" Morgan asked.

"In here *snort oink*," he called from the bathroom. The hot water was running, and Sam was leaning over the sink with a towel draped over his head, breathing in clouds of steam.

"Is that, um, helping?" Morgan asked.

"I think it is, *snort snort*. It's getting better."

"Don't worry," Gretta said to Morgan. "I told you it's nothing. It's just a side effect of the pig's bladder. It'll be gone soon."

"Remember when I had whooping cough? *Snort oink*. Mom made me breathe steam like this," Sam said.

He stood up and took the towel off. "It's working."

"See. It's already wearing off. I told you it was nothing," Gretta said calmly as they went downstairs. "In a few more minutes he'll be absolutely fine. Trust me."

"If you say that one more time. . . ." Morgan said.

"Oh quit being such a glowergrim. And now will you please let me get back to work? I really don't appreciate these constant interruptions."

From the Journal of Gretta Fleetwing

I've had a totally brilliant idea! If I really want to understand humans, what better way than to become one? Just temporarily, of course! Fly a mile with their wings, and all that sort of thing, although in this case I guess it would be walk a mile in their slippers-ha-ha! (Hope I don't really have to walk a mile!)

I think I won't tell Morgan about this yet. I'll surprise her. What fun it will be!

Morgan's emotional stability continues to worry me. What a wingstorm out of a whistle she made about the snorts! I mean, who gets upset about a little case of the snorts? Sammy didn't seem worried at all. And what a darling little trowling he was-well, not little, hardly little. He is quite attractively tall-but he really was absolutely darling and full of energy!

And as it turned out, he didn't need my Restore drops after all. Apparently he was able to reconstruct the missing part of the game. He made it even better, so it all turned out fine.

I've decided that I should become a human in time to go to the dance at Morgan's school. Last time I visited

Morgan, there was a dance; but I was fairy-sized and couldn't have any fun. Plus, as usual, I spent the whole night trying to extract Morgan from yet another situation she had managed to get herself into.

This time things will be different.

I told Tuti about my plan to become a human, and she thinks it's a terrific idea. She brought up some very good points, and I realize I have many details to work out before I put my plan in motion.

Things to consider:

1. Outfit for dance!
2. Red heels or black pumps?
3. Are human boys (Sammy in particular) better dancers than elves? (Let us hope so! Surely they cannot be any worse.)

Speaking of elves, Tuti says that Bristle is missing me terribly, which I find slightly hard to believe, since he hasn't even tried to call me one time. I mean, how difficult is it to point his wand at his cell phone? Tuti says it's because he knows I won't answer, which is correct. But still I would at least appreciate the effort. Tuti says he is trying to respect my request that he leave me alone for a while. Hmm. Too bad he never bothered to respect my requests when we were dating. Tuti also said that troll Jasmine has been buzzing around him, but he's not paying any attention to her. I should hope not. An elf would have to be truly desperate to go after her. The outfit she had on the day I left, well, words really can't describe its complete ugliness. Does she not know that when you have legs the size of pinecones, you really want to avoid minirobes! Honestly, someone should help her.

Speaking of legs like pinecones, I think I've put on a few ounces myself. I have to say that Sally really is one excellent cook. How can a fairy resist? I think I need some exercise. Let's see, what did I do with that tube of Jammin' Juice? Oh I remember. I left it on Morgan's desk. As soon as her father leaves, I'll get it and then I'll do an extra-strenuous workout!

Chapter Five

"I'll be coming in to school tomorrow for a conference with your guidance counselor," Morgan's father said when he came upstairs later that night. He sat on the edge of Morgan's desk.

"Really? Tomorrow?" Morgan said, surprised. "I thought the conferences were next week."

"Yes, but I spoke with Ms. Thomas, your counselor, and asked if we could meet tomorrow before Sally and I go away. Remember? Lorelei will be staying with you guys while we're gone. I wanted to do it before we go."

"Will I be in the conference?" Morgan asked.

"Of course. Tomorrow at three-thirty. In Ms. Thomas's office. You know where it is?"

"I think so. I'll find it," Morgan said.

"Okay then. Well, I'll let you get on with your homework." He stood up to leave and then noticed a spot on the side of his pants. "Hmm. I must've sat in something," he said, rubbing at the spot.

"'Night, Dad," Morgan said.

"'Night, honey." He kissed her good night and went back downstairs.

The minute he was gone, Gretta popped out of the dollhouse and flew over to Morgan's desk. "Have you seen my tube of Jammin' Juice concentrate?" she asked Morgan. "I'm sure I left it on your desk." She flew around the desk and then stopped on the side by the door. "Tsk. Look at that. Someone squashed it." She picked up the little tube, which was about the size of a pushpin and was now flattened. "What a waste. It was a brand new tube."

Morgan stared at it. "Uh-oh. I think my father sat on it."

"He didn't touch any of it, did he?" Gretta asked, frowning.

"It left a spot on his pants, and he rubbed the spot with his fingers. Why?" Morgan asked.

Gretta folded her lips together. "Hmm."

"Gretta. What?" Morgan demanded.

"Nothing, nothing. Don't get your wings in a flap. It'll be fine."

"What is Jammin' Juice?" Morgan asked. "What does it do?"

"Oh, Jammin' Juice is good for all kinds of things. I was going to use it for my workout." She patted her stomach. "With all that great food of Sally's, I've put on a few ounces. I wanted a good workout."

"So how does it work?" Morgan asked.

"Well, you put some in water and splash a little on your legs and arms; and the minute you hear music, you just have to dance!"

"But it's for fairies, right? It probably wouldn't work for humans, would it?" Morgan asked.

"Actually it probably will. See, humans are much more susceptible to our spells and potions than we are. Fairies have a kind of natural immunity because we're exposed so much more than humans," Gretta explained. "And, of course," she looked sadly at the flattened empty tube, "this was the concentrate."

"Gretta, you're telling me my father's going to start dancing every time he hears music?"

"Quit worrying, Morgan. It won't last forever, and he could use a little exercise!"

"How long does it last?" Morgan asked.

"Just about an hour or so."

"Oh. Well, that's no problem then," Morgan said, relieved.

"For fairies, that is," Gretta added.

"My father is not a fairy, Gretta."

Gretta let out a peal of laughter. "Morgan, you're as funny as a noggle in a bog."

Morgan took a deep breath. "How long will it last for a human, Gretta?" she asked patiently.

"There are so many variables here. It could be an hour or two. It could be longer." She shrugged. "There's just no way to tell. But it won't be longer than twenty-four hours."

"Oh great. This is just great," Morgan moaned.

"Well, you certainly can't blame me for this," Gretta told her. "He's the one who sat on it."

"You realize he's coming to my school tomorrow," Morgan said.

"Oh Morgan, don't be such an old glower-grim. It'll be fine."

"Gretta, have you ever seen my father dance?" Morgan asked.

From the Journal of Gretta Fleetwing

Well, no workout for me. If this keeps up I'll be as round as a ballybog soon. And honestly, these humans! Morgan's father heedlessly squashes an entire tube of Jammin' Juice (the concentrate, no less), and all Morgan can think about is her school conference. And she actually blames me—I am not making this up—for all of this!

Well, I must admit, I can understand why Morgan is worried about her father's visit to her school. As she pointed out the thought of him dancing is pretty horrifying. To give you a clue, he kind of reminds me of Cicero, Tuti's pet praying mantis, if Cicero were six feet tall and wore glasses. I've never seen Cicero dance, but, well, you get the idea.

Tuti just called and said that nixie Jasmine has been going to all of Bristle's games and telling him what a wonderful player he is. Grrr! It tilts my crown just thinking about it! And last night she went to his castle and brought him some ambrosia cakes! Can you even imagine? Bristle told her he doesn't like ambrosia cakes (though I happen to know he does), so she went home and ate them all herself! Ha. Just what she needs. She's already the size of a *grapefruit!* I'm surprised she can get off the ground without breaking her wings! And what a conniving gwrach she is, trying to steal my boyfriend when I'm trying to do important work that someday will benefit the kingdom!

Oh, and Bristle told Tuti to tell me he hasn't called because I told her to tell him not to. He knows if he did call I wouldn't answer (which I wouldn't), and if I did answer, I would tell him he shouldn't have called because I told Tuti to tell him not to. So he hasn't. But still. If he was away I would call him even if he did tell me not to.

But he did write me a little note. And he gave it to Tuti to give to me. I'm going to meet her in the morning to get it. And since I'll be meeting her, I've asked her to bring along some Jammin' Juice antidote for Morgan to use on her father.

My plan is this: Since Morgan doesn't seem to want me to come to school with her for some reason (who can fathom the whims of humans?), I've decided to go undercover. I will wear my fog cap and thus be invisible, even to Morgan. I will follow her to school in the morning to see how to get there. Then I will leave to meet Tuti, procure the antidote-and Bristle's note-and of course get the latest on the Bristle/Jasmine situation, and then go back to Morgan's school.

This will give me an excellent opportunity to pursue my research. Now that I am doing a whole chapter on schools, I need lots of material and lots of facts. Humans love facts. The Elder Fairies like them, too. I want to be very factual and convincing because I know the Elder Fairies will accuse me of exaggerating and making things up.

Of course I have to say that *no one* would believe some of the things that go on at FGTA. Like the time Madame Milkweed's robe got snagged on a thorn and she flew off, but her robe stayed behind. I am not making this up. It was too funny! Except none of us could get the image of Madame Milkweed in her fairy-skins out of our minds for ages-not a pretty sight, shudder, shudder. But what a noggle in a bog! It still twirls my wand just thinking about it.

And then there is poor old Professor Winkle who *cannot* keep his crown on his head. Honestly I can't tell you how many times we have found that thing hanging from a twig or lying in a dew puddle. And tarnished? Hades, if one of us students went around with our crowns looking like that-well-dungeon days for us! Honestly has he never heard of Crowns-a-Glow? But of course we students are only allowed to wear our everyday crowns to school, anyway. Only the teachers get to wear their precious crowns. It's so unfair!

Ah well, I better get to bed because tomorrow is a very busy day. Can't wait to see Tuti and get Bristle's note! I must admit, I do miss him just a bit.

Chapter Six

Morgan was waiting in the lunch line when a girl behind her said, "Hey. Weren't you in the Green Team meeting yesterday?"

Morgan turned. "Yeah. You were, too, weren't you? Are you going to join?"

The girl nodded. "I think so. It sounds okay. You can count it as a PE class. I hate PE. I'd much rather plant flowers and save the environment than look like a total dork, trying to play volleyball. By the way, I'm Fiona Jones. You're Morgan, right?"

"Right. Morgan Yates."

"So this is your first year here, right?" Fiona asked.

"First semester. We started in January," Morgan explained.

"Oh wow. It must be rough coming in the middle of the year," Fiona said.

Morgan shrugged. "I like Culver and all, but I kind of miss my old school."

Fiona nodded sympathetically. "No doubt. I'd hate to switch in the middle of the year." Fiona took a sandwich and fries and was getting her drink when another girl came up to her and said, "Fiona, come and sit with Eric and me. You never sit with us anymore. We're over by the mural."

"Okay," Fiona said.

When the other girl had left, Fiona said, "That's Sadie. She's my best friend, but ever since she started going out with Eric, I hardly ever see her. It bites." She took a cookie from the dessert station and picked up her tray. "Hey, you want to sit with us? If you're there I won't feel so much like a third wheel, if you know what I mean."

"Sure," Morgan said. She followed Fiona to one of the smaller tables on the other side of the cafeteria, and Fiona introduced her to Sadie and Eric.

"Are you guys trying out for the play tomorrow?" Fiona asked.

"I want to," Sadie said.

"Not me," Eric said, shaking his head.

"Oh, Eric." Sadie frowned at him. "It'll be fun."

"Just what I want to do is put on tights and a toga, and prance around spewing Shakespeare," Eric said.

"Umm, first of all, this play is *Much Ado About Nothing*, not *Julius Caesar*, so I doubt you'll be wearing togas," Fiona said.

Eric shrugged. "Whatever. Shakespeare's Shakespeare."

"Well, yeah," Fiona said. "But *Julius Caesar* takes place in ancient Rome, like maybe 1,500 years before Shakespeare's time. And it's historical. *Much Ado About Nothing* is a comedy."

"Whatever," Eric mumbled.

Morgan was impressed. Fiona was smart.

"Anyway," Sadie said, "the chances of me getting a part are slim to none. There aren't that many parts, and most of them will probably go to the ninth-graders."

"Yeah. We might get chorus, though. I'd be happy with that," Fiona said. "I'm definitely going to try out."

"You'll get a part, Fi," Sadie told her. Looking at Morgan she said, "Fiona's a terrific actress. She always gets parts."

"Are you going to try out, Morgan?" Fiona asked. "You should."

"I don't know. I'd like to, but I haven't done much acting."

"You gotta start somewhere," Fiona told her.

They were finishing lunch when Eric said, "Looks like the jocks and the techies are getting into it again."

Sam and his friends were sitting at a table near Morgan's, and a few tables away sat a bunch of jocks.

Sam and his friends were huddled around James's laptop when an orange, thrown by someone at the jocks' table, landed with a loud thump on the computer keyboard.

"Hey! Watch it, birdbrain. This is a brand new computer," James shouted.

"Ooh! A brand new computer. Next time I'll aim for your brain instead."

"At least he has a brain, unlike you, Hanson," Sam called.

"You're hilarious, Leighton. So funny I'm like,

paralyzed with laughter," one of the other jocks said, throwing a chocolate-chip cookie at Sam.

Sam caught it and threw it back. "Thanks for sharing, but I wouldn't want to deprive you. Your next feeding might be a while."

"Maybe you want a little milk with your cookies, huh, tech boys?" Todd Hanson said. He picked up a milk carton and threw it toward Sam's table. But the carton made a U-turn in midair; and before Todd could duck, it came back and poured itself over his head. The cafeteria erupted in laughter and applause.

"Nice throw, Todd-o," someone yelled.

Todd stared at the tech table. "How did they do that?" he asked. Brian Gains, who was sitting next to Todd, grabbed an apple. But before he could throw it, Todd's baloney sandwich smacked him in the face.

"What'd you do that for?" Brian asked.

"I didn't," Todd said.

"Then who did?"

"I don't know, but I'm not sticking around to find out." He grabbed the remains of his lunch and raced out of the cafeteria.

"Wow. That was cool. I've never seen anyone

get the best of Todd like that. I wonder who it was. Can anyone see?" Eric said.

"Someone at the tech table, I think, but I couldn't see who," Sadie said.

"I'll ask Sam," Morgan said. "He's my step-brother."

She caught up with Sam as he left the cafeteria. "Sam, hey! What happened back there?"

Sam laughed. "I don't know really. Todd tried to throw a carton of milk at me but hit himself with it instead. It was a beautiful moment."

Morgan introduced Fiona, Sadie, and Eric.

"That was cool," Eric said. "Way to go, tech boys." He put his fist out, and Sam met it with his own.

"Those trolls are not going to insult Sammy and get away with it. Not while this fairy is around," a voice whispered in Morgan's ear.

"Gretta!" Morgan whispered. "What are you doing here?"

"What?" Fiona asked.

"Oh, uh, nothing. It's just, I gotta go. I'll see you later, Fiona." She raced out of the cafeteria and down the hall. When there was no one around, Morgan stopped and said, "Gretta, I told you not to come. How did you even get here?"

"I flew, of course. How do you think I got here?"

"Look, Gretta, I'm having enough trouble—" Before she could finish a door opened, and Ms. Thomas, the school counselor, came out. She looked at Morgan and said, "Hello, there. You're Morgan Yates, aren't you?"

"Yes. Hi, Ms. Thomas," Morgan said.

"I'll be seeing you and your father this afternoon, won't I?" the counselor asked.

Morgan nodded.

Ms. Thomas glanced up and down the hall. "Is everything all right, Morgan?" she asked. "I thought I heard you talking to someone, but you appear to be alone."

"Yes. I was, um, practicing lines for the play," Morgan told her.

"Oh how nice!" Ms. Thomas beamed at her. "I'm so glad you're going to try out. It's a great way to get involved."

The bell rang, and Morgan said, "Well, I better get to class, Ms. Thomas."

"Yes. I'll see you this afternoon, Morgan," the counselor said, walking away.

"Gretta," Morgan whispered when they were alone again, "I'm about to be late. You better go home. If you got here on your own, you can get back home on your own."

"Well, I'm certainly not going to stay where I'm not wanted," Gretta snapped. "But I did think you might want this." She held out a little vial of powder. "It's the antidote for the Jammin' Juice. Just in case."

"Really. Oh that's excellent, Gretta," Morgan said, taking the little vial. "What do I do with it?"

"Ideally you sprinkle it in his ears, but that could be difficult, given the sitch. My advice is to sprinkle it on a wool scarf and have him wear it around his neck, as close to his ears as you can get it," Gretta said, and with that she disappeared.

At three twenty-five Morgan raced down the hall to Ms. Thomas's office. She'd found a wool scarf in her locker and sprinkled the antidote powder on it, but she hoped she wouldn't have to use it. She wanted to get to Ms. Thomas's office first to make sure there wouldn't be any music. She knocked on the door, and Ms. Thomas called, "Come right in."

"Hi, Ms. Thomas," Morgan said.

"Hello there, Morgan. You're right on time. Have a seat."

Morgan looked around the room. No music; no radio in sight. As long as nothing came over the loudspeaker, it should be okay. She sat down in one of the chairs Ms. Thomas indicated, just as her father appeared in the doorway.

"Hello, Mr. Yates," Ms. Thomas said. "Come in, please. Morgan is already here, as you can see."

He came in and shook hands with Ms. Thomas. "Thank you for making time for us today, Ms. Thomas. I know how busy you must be." He sat down next to Morgan.

"We're always happy to meet with parents, Mr. Yates. And we do like to check in with the families of our new students. You said you had some concerns about Morgan's adjustment here at Culver?"

"Yes. Coming to a new school in the middle of the year has been difficult for her," he explained. "Morgan loved her old school."

"Well, you must be pleased that she's trying

out for the play. Drama is such a wonderful outlet, I think," Ms. Thomas said.

"She is?" her father said, looking at Morgan.

"Yes. She hasn't shared that with you?" Ms. Thomas seemed surprised.

"No." Her dad turned to Morgan. "She told us about the newspaper and the Green Team. I had no idea you liked drama, Morgs."

"Well, actually I just kind of decided today," Morgan told him. "On the spur of the moment, sort of."

"Well, that's great," her father said heartily. He looked at Ms. Thomas and said, "There have been a lot of changes for her lately. You know that I recently remarried."

Ms. Thomas nodded. "So I understand." She began to talk about stress related to change, and Morgan and her dad listened. Then through the open window, Morgan heard rap music. She saw her father's feet start tapping, and he began to bounce in his chair. Morgan jumped up. "I'm so cold. Do you mind if I close the window, Ms. Thomas?" she asked.

"Go right ahead, Morgan. It was stuffy in here earlier, but it is getting a bit chilly now."

83

Morgan leaped across the room and slammed the window shut, just as her father was about to stand up. When they could no longer hear the music, he slumped back down in his chair, and Ms. Thomas went on talking about stress.

Everything was fine until, across the hall, the school chorus began practicing for the Valentine's Day concert. The first song was "All You Need Is Love," and Morgan saw her father begin swaying in his seat. "Dad, how's that cold of yours?" she asked quickly. "Look, I brought you this scarf." She jumped up, holding out the scarf. "Why don't you put it on? Here, let me help." She wrapped the scarf around his neck and pulled it up so it covered his ears. He stopped dancing, but he looked at her strangely.

"Well, thank you, Morgan. That's very thoughtful, but I really don't need a scarf right now." He unwrapped the scarf and took it off. He began snapping his fingers and bouncing in his seat, and was halfway out of his chair when Morgan jumped up and pushed him down and wrapped the scarf around his neck again. "You know what the doctor said, Dad."

Ms. Thomas said, "Well, this has been most

enlightening. The family dynamics are very interesting. Before your father's marriage, it was just you and your father, wasn't it, Morgan?" she asked.

"Yes," Morgan said,

"And you were used to taking care of him, weren't you?" the counselor asked.

"Um, not really," Morgan said.

Ms. Thomas gave her a sympathetic look. "It must be very hard to have to share him with your stepmother."

"No, I—it's fine. Sally's great," Morgan said quickly.

"Perhaps we should meet and talk about this again, Morgan," Ms. Thomas said in a concerned voice. "How would you feel about that?"

Morgan saw that her father was unwrapping the scarf again. She jumped up again and said, "Okay, great, 'cause we really have to go right now." She grabbed her father's arm and yanked him out of his seat. "We're going to be late if we don't leave right now, aren't we, Dad?"

"Thank you so much, Ms. Thomas," her father said, shaking the counselor's hand.

"I'll be in touch, Mr. Yates," Ms. Thomas said, giving him a meaningful glance.

From the Journal of Gretta Fleetwing

Well, let me just say this. It is a very good thing that I went to Morgan's school today, in spite of her protests. I wore my fog cap this morning, so she was unaware that I was following her; and once I learned where her school was, I went to meet Tuti. Not much new on the Bristle and Jasmine sitch, but I got the note that Bristle wrote to me, which wasn't exactly a lengthy epistle. He did draw a little heart (quite nec, really) on the outside of the note and wrote "Bristle and Gretta forever" inside the heart, all of which seemed promising. But when I opened it, all he said was, "Come home soon. I miss you. Love, Bristle." Well, I guess that didn't take up too much of his elf-ball time! It is kind of nec, though. I think this little break was the right thing for us. He will finally see that if he wants me to be his girlfriend, he cannot take advantage of my good nature; and I will not allow myself to be controlled by any elf.

Anyway, Tuti gave me the Jammin' Juice antidote, and I arrived back at Morgan's school just in time for lunch.

I was looking for Morgan when I happened to see Sammy and his friends being attacked by a grakish troll named Toad. Fortunately I was able to step in and come to their rescue. I must say, the expression on that Toad's face when I poured the milk on his head was worth a million wands!

Morgan, of course, was worried about me getting her in trouble, blah-blah-blah. What a nellynit she is. But when I told her about the antidote, her crown lit up.

After lunch she wanted me to go home, but I decided to continue my research. I flew all over the school and took notes on everything.

To listen to Morgan one would think her school really is a gallitrap, but it was actually very nice and quite fun. Some kids were watching TV, others were making potions of some kind, some were singing, others were dancing, and some were playing a game that looked sort of like elf ball. Really it's not half as bad as Morgan makes it sound. In fact it's a lot more fun than sitting back here all alone with absolutely nothing to do and no one to talk to.

I was also able to do some excellent research for my chapter on human geography. I listened to some kids who were studying for a geography test, and I took very thorough notes. Tuti called several times during the study session so I may have missed a few things, but fortunately I already know a lot about all of this. And I've been studying Morgan's notes as well. The ones she calls her doodles are particularly helpful. Anyway thanks to my prior knowledge and all this studying, my chapter on human geography is coming along very well, as you can see from the following:

Geography of the Human World

The human world is divided into five main sections: America in the west; Africa in the south; Asia in the east; Arctic in the north; and Australia (also called Atlantis), which is down under. Note that they all begin with the letter "A." This is so they will be easy to remember.

America has lots of people because the land there is free and because there aren't many dangerous animals like lions and tigers and bears. However, there are many dogs because dogs and men are best friends.

Africa is very hot and is mostly jungles and deserts. It doesn't have as many people because there are many man-eating animals like lions, tigers, dragons, dinosaurs, and rhinosaurs (giant unicorns).

Arctic is very cold and is all ice and snow. Not many people live there, and those who do live in castles made of ice and glue called i-glues. There are also polar bears, penguins, and some big-footed giants called yeti.

Asia? Note to self: Research Asia.

Because Australia (also called Atlantis) is under water, only mermaids, mermen, whales, fish, and sea creatures live there.

Zeus. I never realized how exhausting researching and writing a book is.

Oh. Here comes Morgan. Finally! I'm dying to find out how the conference went. For Morgan's sake I do hope the antidote worked. Although the thought of her dad dancing down the halls of her school is really too funny!

Well look at that. She's gone out again already, taking her pooch for a walk. Didn't even bother to say hello or to thank me! I ask you!

Chapter Seven

As soon as Morgan got home, she snapped
Hattie's leash on her and took her out for a walk.
Talk about stress! If she hadn't been stressed
before, she sure was now, after that meeting.

But at least she'd met some nice kids. She
liked Fiona and Sadie and Eric. Finally she would
have something good to tell Ellen when they
talked on the phone.

She and Hattie walked down the block with
Hattie stopping now and then to sniff.

As they were walking by the Saunders' house,
a boy with a golden retriever on a leash came
down their front walk. As they got closer Morgan saw that it was Duncan Saunders. When
Hattie saw the other dog, she strained on her

leash to say hello, so Morgan stopped. The golden came over to Hattie, and they sniffed each other, wagging their tails like old friends. "Hattie likes to make friends with every dog she sees," Morgan said, smiling.

The boy nodded. "Joe does, too." He looked at Morgan. "You go to Culver, don't you?"

Morgan nodded. "You do, too, right?"

"Afraid so," he said.

"I just started there last month. When we moved," Morgan told him.

"Ah. That explains why you still seem like a reasonable human being. But don't worry. It won't be long till you're warped and twisted like the rest off us Culverites."

Morgan laughed. "As bad as that?"

"You have no idea," he said, shaking his head with mock sadness. "No, actually it's an okay place. You like it so far?"

The dogs were straining on their leashes, and Morgan and Duncan fell into step together behind them. "I'm still getting used to it. I miss my friends at my old school and . . ." She shrugged.

"Yeah, that's rotten, switching midyear."

"Kind of," Morgan agreed. "Are you in ninth grade?" she asked.

"Yup. Come June I'm outta there," he said. "I'm Duncan, by the way. Duncan Saunders."

"I'm Morgan. We live in the last house on the right." She waved toward their house. "So, do you live with your grandparents?" she asked, nodding at the big house.

"No, but they're away for a week, so I get to take care of Joe." When Joe heard his name, he looked back at Duncan and wagged his tail. "Yes, Joey, we're talking about you," Duncan said. "He's a sweet dog. I wish we could bring him to our house while they're away, but we have two cats and an eleven-year-old dachshund. Joe doesn't get that he's like, five times bigger than they are; and they get seriously annoyed when he tries to play with them and ends up squashing them."

"Aww. Poor Joe. He's a sweetie," Morgan said, smiling.

"He is. He's a good boy. Not the sharpest knife in the drawer, but he is a sweetheart. And of course my grandparents think he's a dog prodigy."

"Hattie seems to like him," Morgan said.

"So you've met my grandparents?" Duncan asked.

"They came to dinner a few nights ago. Sally, my stepmom, is a caterer, and they wanted to try out her cooking."

"Oh yeah. They mentioned that," he said. "They raved about her food. My grandma wants her to cater some big dinner she's having. They're always having dinners."

"Sally's a great cook," Morgan said.

Duncan looked puzzled. "Do you have a brother?" he asked.

"A stepbrother. Sam," Morgan said. "He goes to Culver, too."

Duncan frowned. "My grandfather was talking about a boy with health problems?"

Oh great, Morgan thought. He had heard all about it. "Well, Sam had a sort of a respiratory problem that night," she told him. "Maybe that's what he meant."

"Yeah. That's it," Duncan said. "See, Grandpa has these spells when he honks and wheezes really loudly. It drives my grandmother nuts, and she thinks he does it on purpose to annoy her. He felt bad for Sam. He was really sympathetic."

"Oh well, it's gone now," Morgan said quickly. "And he'd never had it before. It was just some weird allergy or something."

They watched the two dogs happily trotting along together. Duncan asked Morgan what kind of music she liked, and he told her about the rock band he played in. She found herself telling him about her old school, and about Ellen and Sam. He was telling her about his band's newest song when his cell phone rang. He pulled it out and said, "Oh man. I better take this. It's about band practice."

"That's okay. I've gotta head back. Hattie gets tired. Short legs, you know."

Before Duncan could stop her, Morgan turned and walked back toward her house. He answered his phone, said something, and then called, "Hey, Morgan. I'll see you in school."

"Okay. See you. Bye, Joe," Morgan called.

Back home Morgan ran up to her room. "Gretta? Gretta! Where are you? You cannot believe what just happened." Morgan knelt beside the dollhouse.

"It's about time you're back," Gretta said,

coming to the door. "You could have asked me if I wanted to come with you on your walk."

"Sorry," Morgan said. "I was so stressed after the meeting with Dad and Ms. Thomas that I just had to get out of here."

"How did it go? Did you need the antidote?" Gretta asked.

"Umm, it was okay. But listen to this!" Morgan told her about meeting Duncan.

"So he's fetch?" Gretta asked.

"Gorgeous!" Morgan said.

"All right! But Aunty Gretta has to give him her seal of approval. When do I meet him?"

"I don't even know when I'll get to see him again," Morgan told her. "But I hope it'll be soon."

When Morgan got home the next afternoon, there was a note taped to her door that said, "To Hattie." Morgan unfolded the note and read:

Dear Hattie,
Duncan is going to walk me at 5:00 today. Can you ask Morgan to bring you then, too? I hope you can because my

people are away, and it's kind of lonely here. Duncan is okay but not near as pretty as you. Please come.

Your friend,

Joe

Morgan smiled. "Look at this, Gretta. Is that cute or what?"

"What? He has to have his dog ask you on a date? Sounds kind of gimil, if you ask me." Gretta said.

"It's a joke, Gretta. And it's not a date. It's just a walk."

"Whatever. You're going, right?" Gretta asked.

"Are you kidding?" Morgan said. "I'm totally going. I told you, he's one hundred percent hot. And funny, too."

"In that case," Gretta said, "I guess I'll just have to come along and check him out. By the way, who is that ballybog who's been sitting on the couch all day?"

"That's Lorelei," Morgan explained. "She's staying with us while Dad and Sally are away. She works for Sally."

"She's been staring at that TV all day," Gretta commented.

"She always does when she's here," Morgan said. "She's really sweet, though," she added.

Then Morgan frowned. "Look, Gretta, it's really cold out. I think you better stay here. You can see him some other time."

"Oh I don't mind a little cold weather," Gretta told her. "And besides, a walk will do me good. I need the exercise."

"Gretta, I'll be the one getting the exercise. You'll just be riding on my shoulder," Morgan said.

Gretta laughed. "Oh Morgan, you're so funny. Exercise is exercise. We don't need to count raindrops, do we?"

"What is that supposed to mean?" Morgan asked.

"You humans! Honestly." Gretta flew over to the dollhouse. "I'll just go change into my running slippers," she called.

"Better wear your boots," Morgan said. "It's freezing out."

As they went outside Morgan called, "I'm taking Hattie for a walk, Lorelei."

"All righty, Morgan," called the young woman sitting on the couch, watching TV. "Have a good one."

They walked down the block toward the Saunders' house. "There they are," Morgan said. "Look, Gretta, just stay quiet, okay? Please," she whispered. "It's really hard to talk to someone when you're talking to me, too." Hattie strained at her leash when she saw Joe and Duncan, and Morgan waved.

"You got the note?" Duncan said, smiling and coming toward them.

"Yes. Hattie was very excited. And of course she wouldn't want poor Joe to be lonely," Morgan said, patting Joe.

"Ooh yeah!" Gretta said. "He is fetch!"

"So did you have band practice last night?" Morgan asked as they fell into step.

"Yeah, but our drummer was sick, so we didn't sound like much," Duncan said.

"He plays in a band?" Gretta whispered. "You didn't tell me that!"

This was not going to work. Morgan pulled Hattie back. "Just a sec, Duncan. Let me fix Hattie's collar." She knelt next to Hattie and fiddled with the collar. "Gretta, either be quiet or go home. You're ruining it," Morgan whispered angrily.

"Well, excuse me," Gretta cried. "I thought you wanted to know what I think of him."

"I do, but later. Not now," Morgan whispered. She patted Hattie and stood up. "Her collar gets twisted sometimes," she explained to Duncan.

"Humph!" Gretta complained. "I don't see why it matters. He can't hear me."

"But I can," Morgan whispered.

"Well, if you find me so annoying, I guess I better leave you alone," Gretta said, and off she flew.

Morgan was relieved. Now she could concentrate on what Duncan was saying.

They walked and talked until it started to get really dark. When they came back to the gate in front of Morgan's house, Duncan said, "Same time tomorrow?"

"Sounds good," Morgan said. "We don't want Joe to be lonely."

"Right. And he's become very attached to Hattie."

Morgan laughed. She and Hattie ran up the front walk. "See you," Morgan called over her shoulder.

She raced upstairs, hoping Gretta would not be mad still; but when she knocked on the dollhouse, there was no answer. "Gretta?"

All of her things were there, but Gretta was nowhere to be seen.

Morgan finished her homework and was about to call Ellen when she heard Gretta. She rushed to the dollhouse. "Gretta? Is that you? Where've you been? I've been worried about you."

"It's me," Gretta called. "I had to meet Tuti to get something. See, a few days ago I had this crown quake, and now it's almost time to set it in motion."

"A crown quake? What's that?" Morgan asked.

"You know. It's like a really great idea," Gretta said. She came out and sat on the dollhouse step.

"Oh. Like a brainstorm?" Morgan asked.

"Yup. It's the best idea I've ever had. It's brilliant," Gretta said.

"Oh. What, um, exactly is this crown quake?" Morgan asked warily.

"Just something that will help me with my research," Gretta told her.

"Oh. Well that's great, but, um, no magic, right?" Morgan warned.

"Well, none that involves you," Gretta said.

"Gretta. You promised!" Morgan cried.

"Oh stop being such an old glowergrim, Morgan. It'll be fun. Trust me," Gretta assured her. "And anyway I thought you were so worried about me. Aren't you glad I'm back?"

"I *am* glad you're back," Morgan said patiently, "but—"

"And you'll be really glad when you see me tomorrow!" Gretta told her.

"Gretta? What do you mean?"

"You'll know in the morning; and trust me, you'll love it!"

From the Journal of Gretta Fleetwing

My hard work is paying off!

Morgan has finally met some kids she likes at school. I saw them briefly yesterday, and though I can't say I was totally impressed, they seemed decent enough sorts, for humans. And on top of that, she has met this Dog Boy and is absolutely gabbigammish about him. She talks about him nonstop. He is nec enough, I suppose, but not half as fetch as Sammy, if you ask me! Of course, I didn't have a chance to observe him for long because as soon as we met up with Dog Boy, she tells me to fly away! Can you imagine? She begs me to come with her. I bundle myself up like a samogorska, and off we go into the kingdom of ice and snow. And then two minutes after we meet up with him, it's head for the beehive, Gretta. I ask you?

Anyway, he had written her a note, pretending to be his dog (?), which Morgan thought was adorable: but if you ask me, was kind of gimil. I mean, what if Bristle wrote me a note, pretending to be Wilson, his pet weevil? Would I think this was funny and nec? No I would not. In fact I don't think all that much of Wilson anyway, especially after the time he ate a hole in my best robe. And I definitely wouldn't want to date him!

But I will say this, Morgan was very grateful to me for providing her with the antidote! The conference went fine, so once again all of her worries were for naught. And it's clear that my hard work and fairy assistance are helping her, and that is after all why I'm here. That and the research, of course.

Good news on that front, too. Today I found a new way

to expand my research. I decided to join Lorelei, whose job is sitting on the couch and watching TV all day.

Of course, Lorelei doesn't know I am watching with her, but it has been most enlightening! Human TV is very entertaining. Lorelei loves what they call reruns, according to Morgan. My favorite one is *Buffy the Vampire Slayer*. I also like one called *Bewitched* and another called *I Dream of Jeannie*, although I find it very offensive that Samantha and Jeannie are not allowed to use magic. Whoever wrote these shows must have been spending too much time with the Elder Fairies! I am learning a lot about humans, though, and it will be most useful for my book. I never realized that some humans are able to do magic. And some, apparently, live in bottles. Who knew?!

Well, no doubt my surprise will cheer her up. Tonight I will put away my crown and fold up my wings; and tomorrow I will rise like the, like the, well, like whoever it was who rose from its bed of whatever.

Chapter Eight

Morgan felt someone shaking her shoulder. "Morgan! Wake up! Wake up!"

"Huh? What time's—aahhh! Who . . . ?" She sat up, blinking and rubbing her eyes. "G-Gretta? You're . . . b-big!"

"I'm human size! Isn't it great? What do you think?" Gretta stood up and spun around in a circle. "Ta-dah!"

Morgan grinned. "It's—I—gosh. It's kind of hard to get used to, but you look just like a regular kid." And she did. She looked just like herself, was even wearing the same things she usually wore, jeans and T-shirt; but she looked more like a human and less like a fairy. She wasn't wearing her crown, but there was something else different. "Your wings! Where are they?"

"Wings don't grow. They're folded up under my shirt. I can't fly, of course, but I can walk so fast!" She strode around the room, taking big steps. "See!"

"That's great, Gretta," Morgan said. She yawned and looked at the clock. It was 6:50. "So how did it happen?"

"I got the potion from Tuti yesterday. It works overnight."

"How long will it last?" Morgan asked.

"Until I drink the Reversal potion. A few days, I figure. What better way to find out about humans than to be one? But don't worry. By the time your parents come back, I'll be back to fairy size."

"Yeah. That's good," Morgan said. "So everyone can see you now?"

"Right. I'm just like a regular human!" Gretta laughed and spun around again. "So," she went to Morgan's closet and pulled the door open. "What should I wear? You've got to lend me some clothes. And I've got to choose an outfit for the dance."

"The dance?" Morgan said, sitting up. "*You're* going to the dance?"

"Of course!" Gretta cried. "Why do you think I want to be a human?"

"You said it was for your research," Morgan mumbled.

"Well, that too, of course," Gretta said quickly.

"But I don't even know if *I'm* going to the dance," Morgan told her.

"Of course you're going. Why wouldn't you?"

Now that she had met Duncan, Morgan did want to go. But she wasn't sure she wanted Gretta there.

"Of course if you're not going to go, I could always ask Sammy to take me."

"Gretta, Sam hasn't even met you yet. Which reminds me. What are we going to tell him about you?"

"What do you mean?"

"He's going to wonder what you're doing here. He knows all my friends. He'll wonder where you came from all of a sudden."

Gretta frowned. "Hmm. I know! How about we tell him I'm your long lost sister who was kidnapped by an evil warlock, and I've finally escaped and returned to the kingdom?"

"Um, I'm not sure Sam would buy that, Gretta," Morgan said.

"Oh. Well, how about, you met me when we were shopping for clothes; and I needed a place to stay, so you invited me to your house?"

"I don't really think that would work so well, either." Morgan thought for a minute and then said, "I know. I'll tell him I met you when I was at lacrosse camp last summer, up in New York. We'll say that your family may be moving here, so you wanted to visit."

Gretta clapped her hands. "Perfect! Oh, I'm so excited."

"Do you know anything about lacrosse?" Morgan asked doubtfully. "Just in case someone asks?"

Gretta laughed. "Of course I do, silly. That's when you bounce the ball and try to put it in the hoop-thingy, right?"

"No, that's basketball," Morgan told her. "Lacrosse is when you have a stick with a sort of net on it. And you cradle the ball in the net when you run." Morgan paused. "On second thought, just forget it. Probably no one will ask."

"Okay," Gretta said. "Now what should I wear? I want to look like a real human."

"Yeah, well, just remember, real humans can't do spells," Morgan told her.

Gretta laughed and said, "I know that, sili-ffrit. Trust me. I'll make a great human! You'll be amazed at how much I've learned already."

"I'm gonna take a shower," Morgan said, getting out of bed. "You can wear anything I have, except what I'm wearing." She pulled out her new black jeans and a hooded red sweater. "Why don't you try some stuff on?"

Morgan came back to her room ten minutes later to find her clothes flung all over the place, piled on the bed, the floor, the desk. Her closet and bureau were almost empty.

"We can't go to school today!" Gretta cried. She grabbed Morgan by the shoulders. "You have to take me shopping! I need an outfit. I can't go to the dance looking like a farvann. Nothing looks right on me. Nothing!"

"Gretta, I can't skip school," Morgan said. "Do you know what my dad and Sally would do if they found out? Not to mention my teachers?"

"But they won't find out. They're away. How will they ever know?" Gretta asked.

"Believe me, they'll find out," Morgan told her. "Look, I have to go to school, but you don't have to come if you don't want to."

"I don't want to go shopping all by myself," Gretta whined. "And besides, I *do* want to come to school." She flopped down on Morgan's bed. "But what am I going to do about an outfit?"

"Maybe we can stop at some shops after school. But right now help me straighten up this mess, will you?" Morgan said, shoving her clothes back into the bureau.

Downstairs Morgan was relieved to see that Lorelei wasn't up yet, and Sam had already left.

"My first day as a human. This will be excellent for my research," Gretta said as they started to school.

But after only a few blocks, Gretta complained that her legs were tired. "I never knew how tiring walking is. It's a shame humans can't fly." Then she complained that she was hungry and wanted to stop at the bakery. Then she was cold, so Morgan gave her her sweater; and then the sweater itched.

When they got to school, Morgan said, "Here we are. Look, when I introduce you to my teachers, just remember to be polite and respectful, okay?" She took Gretta into the office to register her as a guest.

"Hi, Ms. Ritter," Morgan said. "This is my friend Gretta Fleetwing. She's staying with me and is coming to school with me today."

"Good morning, Gretta. How nice to have you here," Ms. Ritter said.

"Good morning, Your Honor Professor Teacher!" Gretta said. She put her hands together and bowed deeply.

"Um, yes," Ms. Ritter said, smiling. "And where are you from, Gretta?"

"I'm from America," Gretta announced.

"Uh, yes, I . . ." Ms. Ritter said, looking puzzled.

Morgan pretended to laugh. "Gretta's so funny. She's just kidding. She's from New York."

Ms. Ritter chuckled. "Well, welcome to Culver, Gretta. Morgan, just sign this and make sure she stays with you all day."

"Thanks, Ms. Ritter," Morgan said, signing the paper and hustling Gretta out of the office.

Out in the hall Morgan said, "Your Honor Professor Teacher?"

"I was just trying to be respectful. Like you said. I don't want to get off on the wrong wing here."

"Yeah, well, all you have to do is say hi. And you don't need all those titles. Just the name is fine. And no bowing."

"Okay, okay. Stop worrying, you old nelly-nit," Gretta said, giving Morgan a little slap on the arm. "It'll be fun. Just relax."

Morgan rolled her eyes. "Right. Fun."

They were standing right under the hall bell when it went off. Gretta clapped her hands over her ears. "Eeeek! What in the kingdom is that?"

"The bell. We're about to be late." She grabbed Gretta's arm, and they sprinted toward the English classroom. "Let's hope Tomeo's in a good mood today."

Mr. Tomeo was about to close the door. "Ah. Just in time, Morgan. And who is this?"

"This is my friend Gretta Fleetwing. She's visiting for the day."

"How nice. Hello, Gretta. Welcome to Culver." He put his hand out for Gretta to shake, but she just looked at him and said, "Hi, Tomeo."

"It's *Mr.* Tomeo, Gretta," Morgan said, giving her a nudge so she would shake hands. But Mr. Tomeo had given up on the handshake and put his hand up to his forehead.

"Oh. Hello, Mr. Tomeo, sir," Gretta said, standing up straight and saluting him. Morgan swatted her hand down.

Mr. Tomeo said, "Uh, where are you visiting from, Gretta?"

"New York," Gretta said.

"Ah. Manhattan?" he asked.

"New York," Gretta repeated.

Fortunately Shavahn came up to the desk to speak to Mr. Tomeo right then, so he just said, "Well, enjoy your day with us, Gretta."

When they had found their seats, Morgan said, "Will you stop acting like a freak?"

"What do you mean?" Gretta asked.

"First of all, Manhattan *is* New York. Or part of it. And second, you don't salute. We're not in the army."

"Oh. But I saw them salute on TV. It was a

show called *M*A*S*H*. See there's this guy called—"

"Whatever. We have to be quiet now."

Morgan took out her English notebook and tried to concentrate. English was her favorite subject, and she liked Mr. Tomeo. Beside her Gretta squirmed and fidgeted. "These seats are so uncomfortable," Gretta whispered.

"Shhh!" Morgan said.

"How much longer? This is such a snooze."

Morgan glared at her.

"Do you have any nail polish? My nails are a mess."

Morgan rolled her eyes.

Finally English was over, and Morgan hustled Gretta down the hall to world geography. "Look, Gretta, our teacher, Ms. Shively, is pretty cool, so just keep quiet and try to act normal."

"Yes, Mother," whispered Gretta.

Morgan introduced Gretta to Ms. Shively and then took her to her seat.

"Well, she seems nice enough," Gretta whispered, "but what is with those shoes?"

"She's a teacher, Gretta. She's on her feet all day," Morgan said.

"Well, I'm all about comfort, but really, someone should do her a favor and burn those things."

Ms. Shively was pretty old, but she was still nice-looking. She was small and slender and wore long skirts and bright-colored blouses. Her black shoulder-length hair was streaked with gray but in a way that made it seem like a good thing. Ms. Shively was not really a geography teacher. She was a history teacher. Kids who had her for history actually liked the class. She sometimes dressed up like the historical figures they were studying, and she let them dress in historical costumes when they had debates or acted out historical scenes. Ms. Shively was teaching geography because Mrs. Burns, the real geography teacher, was on maternity leave.

Ms. Shively hated the giant DVD/video projector in the geography room. In her history class she never used that kind of technology. Mrs. Burns, on the other hand, loved technology. Her curriculum depended on it.

Whenever they had to use the DVD player, Ms. Shively would wince and sigh and struggle; and then, when she seemed to be on the verge of tears, she would call one of the students forward to help her.

Ms. Shively began pulling the DVD machine out into the middle of the room, her face tense.

"A movie?" Gretta asked hopefully.

"Don't get excited. They can be pretty boring," Morgan whispered.

"Today, class, we'll be watching *Argentina, Old and New*," Ms. Shively told them. "As you watch, think about how Argentina compares to Brazil."

She dimmed the lights, fiddled with the machine, and amazingly enough, it worked. Ms. Shively seemed as amazed as everyone else. She went to her desk and sat down with a sigh of relief.

The film proved to be as boring as Morgan had predicted, and Gretta was soon squirming and sighing.

"How long is this sleeping pill?" she asked.

"Usually about forty minutes," Morgan whispered.

"Hmm," Gretta said. And the next thing Morgan knew, Argentina was gone, and *Buffy the Vampire Slayer* appeared on the screen.

Gretta was smiling happily. "I love this show. Don't you?"

Everyone in the class laughed and cheered, and Ms. Shively jumped up. "My goodness. How on earth did that happen?" She stopped the video, took it out, and inspected it. "It must be picking up the closed-circuit programming somehow." She fiddled with the remote and then put the video back in. Argentina came back, but as soon as Ms. Shively dimmed the lights and sat down, Buffy flashed back on the screen.

Once again everyone laughed and cheered. Everyone but Ms. Shively, who was seriously annoyed. "What is going on with this machine?" she muttered. "I do not understand this." She fiddled with it, and again Argentina came on; but again as soon as she sat down, Buffy was back.

"That's it!" she said, turning the video off. "We'll just have to watch this another day. I'll get Mr. Blinson to look at the system." She switched the machine off and went to her desk. "Now let's talk about the differences and similarities between—"

The screen flashed on, and Buffy

and her friends were discussing their weekend plans.

Ms. Shively jumped up. "I do not believe this!" She ripped the cord out of the wall, and the screen went blank. "Honestly! Okay, back to the subject—"

Once again Buffy appeared. Ms. Shively looked astounded. "But that's impossible; it's not plugged in. How . . . ?" She shook her head. "Philip, please go down to the Tech Services office and ask Mr. Blinson to come up here. Tell him it's an emergency."

"Now students, try to ignore the TV and take out your notebooks."

Everyone tried to do as they were told, but it was impossible.

"This is one of my favorite episodes," Sarah Newland, who was sitting next to Gretta, whispered.

"Mine, too," Gretta whispered.

"Now write down five places you would like to visit if you were to take a trip to Argentina," Ms. Shively told them.

People were pretending to pay attention,

while staring raptly at the TV show. They heard footsteps in the hall, and the screen went blank. The door opened, and Philip came in, followed by Mr. Blinson.

"I'm told you have a video emergency up here, Ms. Shively," Mr. Blinson said.

"Yes—oh. It seems to have uh—But it, it wouldn't . . ." Ms. Shively stared at the DVD player. "I—I don't understand . . ."

Mr. Blinson picked up the unplugged cord. He said nothing, looking from the cord to Ms. Shively. "Now I don't want to insult you . . ." he began.

Ms. Shively took a deep breath. "Mr. Blinson, I am aware that the machine is not plugged in. I unplugged it myself. But it kept on going, showing that—that Buffy show."

Mr. Blinson snickered. "Ms. Shively, you know as well as I do that this machine cannot operate unless it's plugged in. And even then, I can't conceive of how a show like Buffy could come on, unless one of these youngsters is playing a trick of some kind, sneaking in a DVD behind your back and—"

"Mr. Blinson, in my classroom, the students

do not—" Before she could finish her sentence, Buffy was back.

The students laughed and clapped. Mr. Blinson, holding the unplugged cord in his hand, stared.

"But, but . . ." he mumbled.

"You see what I've been saying, Mr. Blinson?" Ms. Shively said, looking pleased at being vindicated.

"But it's not, it's not possible," he said.

"Apparently it is," Ms. Shively said.

"But this can't happen. It's impossible."

" 'There are more things in heaven and earth, Horatio . . .' " Ms. Shively said.

"It's, uh, Bill, ma'am," Mr. Blinson told her.

"Yes, Bill. I was quoting Shakespeare," she said.

"Ah. Well no offense, ma'am, but I don't think Shakespeare can help us here. They didn't even have computers back then."

"Truer words were never spoken, Bill," Ms. Shively said.

At that moment the bell rang, and for the first time ever, the students groaned. "I really want to see the end," someone said.

From the Journal of Gretta Fleetwing

Well, my first day as a human, and so far so good. Morgan was surprised and happy to see me in human form and very excited about bringing me to school and showing me off. I am learning a lot about humans, too. For example, I learned that you only shake hands with your right hand, or is it your left? Silly me, I've forgotten already; but in the scheme of things, does it really matter? I think not. And every morning they do this thing they call Pled Jelly-Dance, which sounds like fun, but it's not really much of a dance. You just stand up and put your hand on your head—or is it on your stomach?—oops, can't remember that, either—and mumble some kind of a spell.

The classes are all very boring, even worse than fairy classes; and I cannot understand what it is they are supposed to be learning. They don't practice spells, or memorize enchantments, or learn anything useful at all as far as I can see. No wonder humans are so pitifully ignorant!

Honestly, you can learn much more simply by watching TV. In the interests of better education, I arranged to have my favorite show, *Buffy the Vampire Slayer*, shown in one of our classes. Of course their teacher did not approve, but I managed to outwit her. Even Morgan had to admit that my spell-making was masterful. Of course outwitting that teacher is nothing to call the castle about. Anyone who would wear shoes like hers clearly doesn't have much under her crown! I wanted to say something to her about those gimil shoes—just a helpful suggestion, but Morgan rushed me out before I could lend my help. One can only do so much.

Tuti called a while ago to find out how my humanization is going and to give me an update on things in the kingdom. She also told me that that jarnvidja Jasmine has started a cheerleading squad and has appointed herself head cheerleader. So now she'll be going to all of Bristle's games and leading cheers at them. Grrr. Just the thought of it makes my wand smoke. Cheerleading does sound like fun, though. According to Tuti they get to wear fetch little skirts and sparkly tops. Hmm. Well, pinecone legs won't look like much in those! And let's hope she's on the bottom if they try one of those pyramid thingies!

When I get home I will definitely join the cheerleading squad. I should probably do some practicing while I'm here. I wonder if Morgan knows anything about cheerleading. Must ask.

Well, it looks as though this boring class is almost over, thank Zeus. Next we have lunch. I'm so excited. I've always wanted to eat in a cafeteria. I can't wait to pick out my food. Morgan said I can have whatever I want. She says the food isn't very good, but still I get to have my own tray and everything. And I am definitely going to sit beside Sammy. Morgan doesn't want me to use spells, so I will rely on my outgoing personality and my fairy charm to attract him. I have no doubt that Sam and Gretta will be an item before lunch is over!

Chapter Nine

At lunchtime Morgan ran into Fiona in the lunch line. "Come sit with us again, okay?" Fiona said.

"Sure. Umm, this is my friend, Gretta. She's visiting from New York," Morgan said.

"From New York? Cool," Fiona said. "See you guys at the table."

"I don't want to sit with her," Gretta whispered when Fiona had left. "I want to sit with Sammy."

"Are you nuts?" Morgan whispered. "I finally meet some cool kids, and I am definitely sitting with them."

"But I need to observe him," Gretta said.

"You can observe him later. We're sitting with Fiona," Morgan told her, "and please try to act halfway normal."

Gretta pouted, but she followed Morgan to Fiona's table and behaved okay until near the end of lunch when Sam came over to their table.

"Morgan, listen, tell Lorelei I'm spending the night at James's, okay?" Sam said.

"Okay," Morgan said.

"No food fights today, huh, Sam?" Fiona asked.

"Nope. Sorry to disappoint you, Fiona," he said, smiling and sitting down next to her.

Gretta dug her elbow into Morgan's arm. Morgan gave her a look but said, "Hey, Sam, this is Gretta, my friend from lacrosse camp. Remember I told you she was coming to visit?"

"You did?" he asked.

"Hi, Sammy!" Gretta said. "I feel like I've known you forever. I've heard so much about you from Morgan!"

"You have?" he asked.

"Of course." Gretta put her chin in her hand and leaned closer to Sam, widening her eyes and batting her lashes. "She told me all about how you build robots and make video games."

"Huh. Well, nice to meet you, Gretta," Sam

said. He turned away from Gretta and back toward Fiona. "So what did you think of that history test?" he asked Fiona.

"Not much. It was impossible," Fiona said.

"No kidding," Sam agreed. "I know I failed."

"Yeah, right. You probably aced it, Sam," Morgan said.

Eric stood up and said, "Later, guys. I'm outta here."

Morgan collected her lunch stuff and stood up, too. "See you at play tryouts."

"Cool. I'm really glad you're trying out," Fiona said, following Morgan. After they had dumped their trays, Fiona grabbed Morgan's sleeve and pulled her back. "Wow. Sam is a hottie. Is he, like, dating anyone?"

"Not right now," Morgan said, smiling.

"Hmm," Fiona raised one eyebrow. "We just might have to change that."

"Go for it, girl!" Morgan told her. She held her hand out, and Fiona slapped it.

"See you later," Fiona called as she took off down the hall.

"Come on, Gretta," Morgan said, heading to class.

"Excuse me, but I do *not* like that girl," Gretta said.

"Who, Fiona? She's great," Morgan said.

"Hmmph. She's a nixie. Practically throwing herself at Sammy," Gretta snarled.

Morgan laughed. "Gretta, get over it. Sam needs a girlfriend, and Fiona would be perfect."

"Well, we'll just see about that."

"Gretta!" Morgan stopped and stared at her. "You promised. No spells. And you've already broken your promise with the whole Buffy thing." Morgan laughed in spite of herself. "That was pretty funny, though."

"Told you I've gotten better," Gretta said proudly.

When their last class was over, Gretta asked, "Are we going shopping now?"

"After play tryouts," Morgan said. "They won't take long, and then we'll go shopping. I promise."

On their way to the auditorium where the tryouts were being held, they passed the gym. A big sign on the gym wall read CHEERLEADERS NEEDED. TRYOUTS TODAY.

"Cheerleaders?" Gretta said in an awed voice. "They have cheerleaders here?"

"Of course," Morgan told her.

"Morgan, I've got to try out. Remember I told you about that awful Jasmine, who's trying to steal Bristle?"

"Yeah, but what does that have to do with cheerleading?" Morgan asked.

"She's started a cheerleading squad, and I'm going to join it when I go home. But I need some practice."

"Do you even know what cheerleaders do, Gretta?" Morgan asked.

"Of course," Gretta assured her. "They wear those fetch little outfits and get lifted up by those nec guys. It looks like such fun! Can we go, Morgan? Please, please, can we?" Gretta begged.

"But Gretta, you won't be here long enough to be on the team. This is just tryouts," Morgan explained.

"I don't care. It will still be fun, and I can learn some routines." Gretta said.

"But I have to go to play tryouts. And I do not want to be a cheerleader," Morgan said.

"So you try out for the play, and I'll try out

for cheerleading," Gretta said, holding her hands out. "It's simple."

Morgan frowned, thinking. She really didn't want Gretta to come to play tryouts. It would be a distraction, and there was no telling what the fairy might do if she got bored. Maybe this was the answer. Morgan nodded. "Okay. You go on in. Pretend you're a student and do what they tell you."

Gretta clapped her hands. "Yes! Oh I'm so excited!"

"Just don't leave the gym," Morgan told her. "Wait here for me, okay?"

Morgan hurried to the auditorium. She took the script that the drama teacher, Mr. Turner, was passing out and looked around for a seat.

"Morgan. Hey, over here." Fiona was waving to her from a row near the front.

"Thanks for saving me a seat," Morgan said as sat down next to Fiona.

When everyone was settled Mr. Turner began to speak. He explained that the actual tryouts would begin next week. Today he just wanted to familiarize them with the play and the characters, explain the ground rules for the production, and go over the rehearsal schedule. He talked for about half an hour and then asked them to sign up for the role they wanted. Fiona signed up for almost every role, but Morgan chose two smaller parts and chorus.

When they were done Morgan hurried back to the gym. She found Gretta in a line with five other kids. The others seemed to know the routine pretty well, and Gretta was trying to follow them but kept messing up. It didn't seem to bother her, though. She was beaming. She jumped and leaped and shouted out the cheer enthusiastically.

Morgan lounged against the bleachers, waiting until the routine was over, glad that Gretta was having such fun. She glanced around the gym, and that's when she saw Duncan Saunders huddled in a corner, talking intensely to Vanessa VanDorren, the captain of the cheerleading team. What was that about? she wondered. Was there something between the two of them?

In a minute Duncan walked off toward the locker room, and Vanessa came over to watch the tryouts from the sideline, not far from where Morgan was standing. Every time Gretta messed up, Vanessa frowned and shook her head, muttering to herself. There was a tub full of melting ice and bottled water near her. Vanessa reached in, grabbed a bottle of water, and opened it, sipping it disgustedly. Finally she blew her whistle and stepped toward the group. She pointed at Gretta and said, "I don't know if you're joking or what, but you are hopeless. Why don't you just leave and let the others get on with it?"

"You mean I can't even try out?" Gretta looked crestfallen.

Vanessa snorted. "Believe me, we've seen all we need to see."

"But can't I just finish the routine? I'm really good on the ending," Gretta said.

Vanessa rolled her eyes. "Look, do us all a favor—"

"Just let her finish, Vanessa. She's not hurting anything," Morgan said.

Vanessa looked Morgan up and down. "Who are you?"

"I'm Morgan Yates. I'm her friend," Morgan said, nodding toward Gretta.

"Well, Morgan Yates, I don't think I really need your input here, so why don't you and your friend just—" but before she could finish, her feet slipped out from under her and she fell backward, landing on her rear end in the tub of melting ice and water.

Gretta threw her pom-poms at Vanessa and said, "I wouldn't be on your cheerleading team if it were the last one in the kingdom." She stomped toward the locker room, turning back for a minute to shout, "And by the way these outfits are so yesterday!"

From the Journal of Gretta Fleetwing

Well, I begin to see that though Morgan definitely has issues, and sometimes she can be a real a boggle-bo, she is crown and wings above many other humans, particularly that vargamor Vanessa.

No doubt Vanessa was jealous of my innate cheerleading abilities and didn't want to have to compete with me, so she tried to throw me out before I even had a chance. I ask you! And when Morgan stuck up for me, Vanessa told her to butt out. That's when I decided Vanessa needed to cool off a bit. Well, I guess that's the last time that Vanessa will mess with Gretta Fleetwing. You should have seen the look on her face when I landed her booty in that icy tub! Ha-ha! It was hilarious. I was a little worried that Morgan might be upset with me, but she totally agreed that Vanessa was asking for it.

Anyway, I am glad I had a chance to practice my cheerleading a bit, and I picked up some great moves. Of course it will all be a lot easier when I am back to fairy size again and have my wings back. I have to admit, being a human is quite exhausting! Having to walk everywhere is not as much fun as you might think.

I must say that in the few short days I've been here guiding her, Morgan has gone from having no friends to having quite a few. At lunch she insisted we sit with her new friend Fiona. (Honestly, I don't know what she sees in this nixie-nocker.) Sammy came over to our table, no doubt attracted by my radiant beauty, and sat down right across from me! Ooohhh! That lit up my crown, as you can imagine! But every time I tried to talk to him, Fiona would foist herself between us and monopolize him. I'm sure this was as irritating to him as it was to me, but of course Sammy is way too polite to tell her to back off. Talk about throwing yourself at a guy! And Morgan encourages her. Poor Morgan. Such a trowling.

Then after Morgan's play practice, we were detained by a boy who wanted to show her his computer game; and then she had to go talk to the newspaper editor. At this rate I'll be going to the dance in my fairy skins!

Ah, here she comes now. Finally we are off to find the perfect outfit for me to wear to the dance. I have no doubt that once Sammy sees me in it, all thoughts of Fiona will fly from his brain, and he will fly to me—although I may have to give the course of true love a bit of nudge, just to be sure! It is, after all, my one chance to attend a human dance, and I do so want to have fun! And of course it will be excellent for my research!

Chapter Ten

"Honestly! I have never in my life been treated like that! Who does that jarnvidja think she is?" Gretta and Morgan had walked several blocks and were almost at the shops, and Gretta was still grumbling about Vanessa.

Morgan knew she had made an enemy of Vanessa, but she didn't care. Gretta had looked so disappointed, she'd had to stand up for her. She was more worried about what Duncan had been doing with Vanessa. Vanessa might be mean, but in the looks department, she was perfect, and guys had to love her. Morgan didn't stand a chance against someone like Vanessa.

"Let's try this place," Morgan said when they

came to a shop called Lilly's. "They have some cute things."

"Ooh. I love that outfit in the window," Gretta said.

They went inside and began combing through the racks of skirts and pants. When Gretta had chosen several things to try on, Morgan found a salesperson to let them into a fitting room. "My name is Sylvia," the young woman said, unlocking the fitting-room door. "Just let me know if you need anything."

"What about you, Morgan? Aren't you getting anything?" Gretta asked.

"I may try on some things, but I'm not going to buy anything today," Morgan said. "I went shopping with Sally last week."

Gretta finally settled on a skirt and slinky top that looked great on her.

"Perfect. Go for it," Morgan told her.

"So how did they work for you?" Sylvia asked when they came out of the fitting room.

"Fine, thanks," Gretta said.

"Would you like me to wrap them up for you?"

"Why, thanks," Gretta said. "That's so nice." She followed the young woman over to the counter.

"So how do you want to pay for these?" Sylvia asked as she wrapped the clothes.

"Pay?" Gretta said.

"Will you be using a credit card?"

"Credit card?" said Gretta.

"We do take personal checks, but we'll need to see some ID," Sylvia explained.

"Umm, Morgan?" Gretta called.

"What's up?" Morgan asked, coming over to the counter.

Gretta grabbed Morgan's arm and yanked her away from the counter. "This boggle-bo says we have to pay," Gretta told Morgan.

"Yeah. Duh," Morgan said.

"Well, how do we do that?" Gretta demanded.

"Don't you have money?" Morgan asked.

"Of course I don't have money. I'm a fairy."

"Gretta, how did you think—" Morgan began.

"I know. I'll put a sleep spell on her and we'll just—"

"No!" Morgan shouted.

"Well, what does money look like? I could try to conjure up some."

"That would be counterfeiting. It's illegal."

Gretta sighed and rolled her eyes. "Well how do humans get money then?"

"We earn it, Gretta. You know. By working."

"How dwergish! Honestly, you humans!"

"Excuse me, ladies? Is there a problem?" Sylvia asked.

"Yes," Morgan said. "We, uh, have to go. Sorry." Morgan took Gretta's hand and pulled her out of the store. "Look, Gretta, you can't go around putting spells on people and stealing things, or conjuring up counterfeit money."

"But I need something to wear to the dance," Gretta said.

"You can borrow something of mine," Morgan told her.

"But I really liked that skirt. I want something new!" she whined, sounding like a little kid. Morgan took pity on her. "Look, I have an idea. I've got a babysitting job this evening, and I'll make some money. Tomorrow we'll go to Twice Sold Tales. It's a consignment shop, but you can find cool stuff there. And it's much less expensive."

Gretta's eyes lit up. "Babysitting? I've heard about that. You sit on the eggs to hatch the babies, right?"

"No, human babies aren't—well, umm—never mind. Babysitting is when you help parents by watching their kids so the parents can go out."

"Oh. So all we have to do is watch some trowlings? That sounds easy. I'm sure I'll be very good at it. Look how well I watch TV!"

"Right," Morgan said. "But you don't have to come, Gretta. It's so boring, and these kids can be pretty bratty. You really don't want to come."

"But what will I do?" Gretta asked. "Sammy said he was going out. Maybe I could go with him?"

"No," Morgan said quickly. "He's going to James's house. I don't even know where it is. But you can watch TV with Lorelei."

"She's as boring as a pumphut. I am not sitting around with her. Either I get to come with you, or I'm calling Sammy. I'm sure he'll come and get me," Gretta said.

Morgan decided she better take Gretta along. At least that way she could keep an eye on her, and there was no telling what she might do if she was left alone and angry.

"Okay, you can come with me. But no funny stuff, Gretta. I mean it," Morgan warned.

When they got home Morgan was about to snap on Hattie's leash to go to meet Duncan and Joe, but Lorelei called to her. "Morgan, your friend Duncan called and asked me to tell you that he won't be able to make it this afternoon. He got held up at school, and his mom took care of Joe."

Morgan's heart sank. Held up at school? By Vanessa? Well it was pretty obvious she wasn't going to have any date for the dance. Her only hope was that maybe she would run into him at the game tomorrow.

Later as they walked to the Stoddards' house, Morgan said, "Look, Gretta. Let me do the talking to the parents. Just say hello and nothing else, okay?"

When they arrived at the house, Morgan said, "This is my friend Gretta Fleetwing, Mrs. Stoddard. Is it okay if she helps out tonight?"

"Hello, Gretta. So nice of you to help. You may soon regret it," she joked. "The twins are insane tonight," she went on, looking at Morgan. "I don't know what's gotten into them."

As if on cue Roddy came barreling around the corner, wearing a towel tied around his shoulders like a cape and waving a Luke Skywalker light sword. "Who's she?" he demanded, pointing the light sword at Gretta.

"This is Gretta," Mrs. Stoddard said. "She's a friend of Morgan's, and she'll be helping out tonight."

"Ha!" Roddy shouted, and he raced off.

Next they heard a clump, clump, clump, and Marco appeared, wearing a huge pair of black work boots and wielding a plunger. "I lotht a tooth," he said, showing Morgan his teeth.

"That's great, Marco. Did the tooth fairy come?" Morgan asked.

"Yeth. Thee took my tooth and left me a thil-ver dollar."

"Cool!"

"Who'th thee?" he asked, pointing the rubber end of the plunger at Gretta.

Mrs. Stoddard introduced Gretta.

"Ha!" shouted Marco, and he clumped off.

"He loves those boots of Tom's," Mrs. Stoddard said. "He wanted to wear them to bed last night. I hope he won't try that again tonight." She blew a strand of hair off her forehead and went on. "They've had dinner, and they each can have two cookies for dessert. Bed at eight-thirty and only one hour of TV."

Morgan nodded.

"Our cell numbers are on the refrigerator, if you need us. We should be home by eleven," Mr. Stoddard told them.

They kissed the boys and left.

"So. Now we watch TV?" Gretta asked.

"No, now we keep them from destroying the house and killing each other," Morgan said.

The twins zoomed around the corner. "Thop, thief," Marco shouted, bopping his brother with the rubber end of the plunger. "He'th got my thilver dollar." Morgan caught Roddy and swung him up, out of Marco's range.

When they had solved the silver-dollar dispute and settled the twins at the kitchen table with their cookies and some crayons, Gretta whispered, "I can't believe you perpetuate that ridiculous tooth-fairy myth."

"What?"

"As if we fairies would want to keep human teeth. Yuk. It's disgusting!"

"Well, adults don't believe it. It's just for little kids. So they don't get upset about losing a tooth," Morgan explained.

"Humph. I think you should tell them the truth," Gretta muttered.

"Oh Gretta. They'll find out soon enough. Let them alone."

"I need the red crayon," Marco yelled, trying to grab it from Roddy.

"I'm using it," Roddy said.

"I was uthing it. I only put it down for a thecond."

"You know, Morgan, I could make this much easier. A silencing spell is one of the simplest—"

Morgan looked at Gretta. "Don't even think about it."

"But—"

"Gretta, I am not kidding. They'll be going to bed soon, anyway."

Roddy threw the red crayon, and it hit Gretta on the forehead.

"Come on, guys, your mom said you could

watch TV for an hour. Let's go see what's on," Morgan suggested.

The twins raced out of the kitchen into the den. "Dibs on the big chair," Roddy shouted.

"I mean it, Gretta," Morgan whispered. "If you want me to take you shopping tomorrow, you better not try anything."

"So we're just supposed to sit here and let them torture us?" Gretta asked.

"That's what they pay us for," Morgan told her.

Gretta frowned. "Humans!"

She pulled out her notebook and began writing furiously.

They watched TV for an hour, and then Morgan took them upstairs. They put their pajamas on and brushed their teeth, and Morgan tucked them into their beds. Then she sat on the beanbag chair between their beds and read them a bedtime story.

Morgan sat up with a jolt. She must have fallen asleep! Both the beds were empty, and the twins were nowhere in sight. She jumped up and raced out of the bedroom. "Roddy! Marcos! Where are you?"

"In here, Morgan," Gretta called from the parents' bedroom.

Morgan looked in and saw Gretta in the middle of the big bed with one twin on either side. "Gretta'th telling uth a thory," Marcos said.

"Go on, Gretta," Roddy said.

"So," Gretta went on, "The mean old varg-amor Vanessa was so jealous of the incredibly talented and beautiful cheerleader Gretta, and so mad that everyone loved Gretta and hated Vanessa, that she decided she would find a way to ruin Gretta's cheerleading career."

Gretta looked up. "Sit down, Morgan. I'm almost finished."

"I hate that dumb old Vanetha!" Marcos said.

"Me too. I'd like to punch her," Roddy said.

Gretta beamed at them. "You two are the most intelligent trowlings I've ever met!"

From the Journal of Gretta Fleetwing

So there we are in this shop. And I have finally managed to find a goss outfit for the dance–a fetch top that looked perfect with my golden curls, and a skirt that showed off my figure beautifully. I would have looked so nymphen in them, if I do say so myself. And then this saleslady with a face like a farvann refuses to let me have the outfit. You would think she'd be flattered that I wanted to wear one of her outfits, but no. She insists that I have to give her something called a credit card. Talk about putting sap on my wings! And of course Morgan wouldn't let me put a sleep spell on her, or simply conjure up some money, or one of these credit cards.

I'm not even sure what a credit card is—some kind of human gold, I suppose. How should I know? At home in the kingdom, my outfits are all spun for me by Nanny Button-crop, my fairy godmaid. I just look through the fashion mags—*Crown and Gown* is my fave, but I like *Stylish Fairy*, too—to show her what I want, and a few minutes later I'm wearing it. A much better system than this complicated buying process that humans do. It's very inconvenient. Today, for example, I actually had to wear the most hideous pair of boots. Believe me, I would rather be caught without my crown than be seen wearing these disasters if I were at home, but Morgan insisted. And I must admit, if I had worn the little pumps I wanted to wear, my tootsies would have been a tad chilly. That's another thing I don't understand about humans. They have no control over the weather! Can you imagine? As much as I complain about the Elder Fairies, I will say that at least they manage to keep the kingdom climate temperate.

So, unbelievably, I still have nothing to wear to the dance, which is tomorrow! Honestly, these humans seem to have no concept of priorities!

Although I suspect that this was Morgan's plan all along, so that she could coerce me into helping her babysit those two trowlings. Fortunately I was there, or who knows what might have happened. Morgan had absolutely no control over them; and she slept the entire time anyway, leaving me to take charge. I must say, they are quite intelligent for human trowlings, though like all humans, totally lacking in discipline.

Tuti called a few minutes ago. She thinks I should come home soon. Bristle is miserable, and Tuti thinks he has definitely learned his lesson. And I do miss him, but I cannot abandon Morgan right now. Can he not see that? There is no way I'm leaving here before the dance-oops-I mean, before I get Morgan out of the gallitrap.

Chapter Eleven

The next day was Saturday, and Morgan and Gretta slept until ten. They were in the kitchen eating breakfast when Sam came home.

"You going to the game?" he asked Morgan.

"Yup. We're going shopping first, though."

"Hmm. Is, umm, your friend Fiona going?" he asked.

"Probably."

Morgan saw Gretta's lips tighten and her nose wrinkle when Sam mentioned Fiona. To change the subject she said, "Gretta's never been to a basketball game."

"Don't they play it at your school in, umm . . . ?" Sam asked.

"Boston," Gretta said.

"I thought it was Brooklyn," Sam said.

"That right. It is Brooklyn," Gretta said. "I forgot for a minute."

"You forgot where you live?" Sam asked, looking at her strangely.

"She used to be from Boston," Morgan said quickly. "I mean, she just moved to Brooklyn. Anyway, we'd better go. We'll meet you at the gym at twelve-forty-five, okay?"

"Sounds good," Sam said, yawning. "I'm going back to bed. We played video games till two AM last night."

"See you later, Sammy," Gretta said.

"I'm, uh, Sam, Gretta."

"Of course you are, Sammy. I know who you are, you sili-ffrit."

"No, I mean . . . never mind. See you at the game," he said sleepily.

Morgan and Gretta went to Twice Sold Tales and found some cute tops and a cool skirt for Gretta. "That's perfect for the dance," Morgan told her, paying for the clothes with the babysitting money they had made.

* * *

They were walking into the gym with Sam when Gretta said, "I'm so thirsty. Does anyone want a drink? I'll go get us some water."

"There's Duncan," Morgan said. She was about to go over and say hi when Vanessa ran up to him. Morgan wasn't going anywhere near Vanessa if she could help it. She saw Duncan nodding, and then he followed Vanessa out of the gym toward the locker room. Her heart sank. That was twice she had seen them together. There must be something going on between them.

Gretta came back carrying two cups of water from the water cooler. "Here we are! Here's yours, Sammy," she said.

Sam took the cup and was about to take a sip when someone called "Hey, Landing!" Sam looked around. "Hold this a sec. I'll be right back." He handed his cup to Morgan.

Morgan held the cup, watching for Duncan to come back so she could go and talk to him. "Gretta, I saw Duncan a few minutes ago. He was talking to Vanessa. And now he's disappeared."

"That farvann probably chased him away. Who can blame him?" Gretta said.

Sam still hadn't come back so Morgan drank the water and crushed the paper cup in her hand.

Someone tapped her on the shoulder, and she spun around. It was the school mascot, clapping his huge hands, his big smiling mask nodding at her. Morgan laughed and said, "Hi, there!" She smiled back at him, and as she looked into his eyes, she thought, Oh look at him, he's . . . he's wonderful!

The mascot motioned for Morgan to come with him, so she followed him through the crowd.

Gretta followed Morgan. "Morgan? Hey, Morgan. Where's that cup of—" She took one look at the empty cup in Morgan's hand. "Morgan. Tell me you didn't drink Sam's water."

"Gretta, it's just water. There's plenty more in the watercooler." Morgan laughed. "Come on. We're going with Kanga. Isn't he great?"

"Who?" Gretta asked.

"Kanga the Culver kangaroo, our mascot." Morgan sighed. "He's so cute, isn't he? And so energetic. Just watch him."

"Morgan?" Gretta was staring at her.

"What? Why are you looking at me like that?"

"Morgan, when you drank that water, umm, was that Kanga nearby?"

But Morgan was following Kanga to the sideline. By the time Gretta caught up to her, Morgan was clapping her hands and dancing along with the mascot.

Gretta grabbed Morgan's arm and pulled her back into the crowd. "Morgan, let's go find Dog Boy. Weren't you going to meet him here?"

"I don't really want to see him right now. I just want to watch Kanga. He's so great, isn't he? I wish I was a cheerleader so I could dance with him." She jumped and danced along with Kanga's cheers.

"You don't want to be a cheerleader, Morgan. Remember what you said yesterday," Gretta said, grabbing her arm.

"I do, though," Morgan told her. "I just want to dance with Kanga."

"Morgan, look." Gretta took her by the shoulders. "Kanga's not real. He's just, just a costume!"

"That's ridiculous," Morgan cried. "You shouldn't say that, Gretta. Kanga is wonderful."

151

"Morgan, that water you drank? It was, well, it was kind of meant for Sam," Gretta told her.

Morgan laughed. "You're still worried about the water? Gretta, there's plenty—"

"No, Morgan, it's just that you've got to go find Duncan."

"Now who's being a glowergrim. I thought you wanted to be a cheerleader?" Morgan said. "And by the way I think you're very mean to say that about Kanga. You know how you hate it when people say fairies aren't real."

Gretta groaned. Sam came over to them and said, "What are you guys doing down here? Come on. Let's go up to our seats. Fiona and Eric saved them for us."

"We'll be up in a few minutes, Sam," Morgan said, waving him away. "We want to watch the cheerleaders."

Vanessa saw Morgan and Gretta standing on the sidelines and gave them a long look of pure hatred.

"Whoa, Morg. What did you do to her?" Sam asked. "She looks like she'd like to murder you."

"She's jealous of me and Kanga," Morgan said.

Sam laughed. "Whatever you say, Morg. I'm going up to our seats. The game's about to start."

When Gretta saw Vanessa's evil look, she said, "That vargamor! Come on, Morgan! Let's show her a thing or two." There were some extra pom-poms lying on the bench near them, and Gretta grabbed a pair for herself and a pair for Morgan.

The team manager shouted, "Everyone off the sideline except players and cheerleaders."

"We're cheerleaders," Gretta said, shaking the pom-poms at him.

The real cheerleaders were executing a complicated dance routine, and Kanga was cavorting back and forth in front of them, clapping and pointing and waving at the crowd. When he saw Morgan and Gretta with their pom-poms, he gestured for them to come out and dance with him.

Gretta took Morgan's arm and they rushed out to join Kanga. He put an arm around both of them and the three of them did a cancan, kicking their legs in unison, and leading the crowd in a cheer, until Vanessa stomped over to them. "What do you think you're doing?" she yelled, ripping the pom-poms away from Morgan and Gretta. "You're not cheerleaders. What are you doing out here? Get off the court now or you'll live to regret it."

"Come on, Gretta. I've got an idea," Morgan said. She turned to Kanga and whispered, "We'll be back." As they left the court Kanga waved sadly and blew them kisses.

"There have to be some extra cheerleading outfits somewhere," Morgan told Gretta, "and we're going to find them." They left the gym and raced to the girl's locker room.

"This is so goss, Morgan." Gretta said happily. "I get to be a real cheerleader at a real game!"

"And I get to be with Kanga," Morgan sighed dreamily.

They found some old outfits in the locker room and changed quickly.

When they got back to the game a few minutes later, Kanga was sitting on the bench and Vanessa was leading an elaborate dance on the sidelines. When Kanga saw Morgan and Gretta in their cheerleading outfits, he stood up on the bench and did a little victory dance, waving for them to come sit with him.

"I told you we'd be back," Morgan said, and Kanga clapped his big paws.

When the half-time whistle blew and the players left the court, Kanga took Morgan's hand in one paw and Gretta's in the other and led them onto the court.

While the cheerleaders worked their routines, doing flips and turning cartwheels, Morgan, Gretta, and Kanga danced, spinning and boogying all over the gym.

"This is the most fun I've ever had," Gretta shouted. "I knew I'd make a great cheerleader! Watch this!" Waving her pom-poms she backed up, took a running start, and flung herself into a cartwheel. She stumbled, missed her step, and slammed feet first into Morgan.

"Oof," cried Morgan. She landed on her stomach and slid into the cartwheeling line of cheerleaders, knocking them down like spinning tops.

The crowd roared, thinking that it was all part of the act. Kanga rushed to the cheerleaders, helping them up one by one, and pretending to dust them off. Finally he came to Morgan. He pulled her up and she threw her arms around him, kissing him on his big rubbery nose. Again the crowd roared. Everyone loved it.

Everyone except Vanessa. She marched over to Morgan and Gretta, her face red with fury. "You cannot wear those outfits! You are *not* part of the squad!" she shouted.

"Yeah, Vanessa. You better have them arrested for impersonating cheerleaders," one of the players joked.

Kanga shook his head and wagged his finger at Vanessa. Then he hugged Morgan, as if protecting her.

The referee's whistle blew, and the second half started. Kanga led Morgan and Gretta to the bench. Even Gretta knew better than to try to join any more cheers.

When Culver's star player made an incredible shot in the last minute of the game and brought them into the lead, everyone was on their feet cheering; and when the buzzer sounded and Culver had won, Kanga threw his arms around Morgan, jumping up and down with her in his arms. Was it her imagination or did he hold her a little longer than he needed to?

The game was over and the gym began

clearing out. Morgan saw Fiona and Sam waiting for her.

"I'd better go," she said, squeezing Kanga's paw.

He nodded. "You'll be at the dance tonight, right?" he whispered.

It was the first time he had spoken, and though she could barely hear him, she thought his voice was beautiful and his words thrilled her.

"Definitely," Morgan said, wishing she didn't have to leave him.

"See you tonight," Kanga whispered, squeezing her hand between his paws before he let her go.

When Morgan and Gretta caught up to the others, Fiona put her hand out for a slap. "That was awesome. What an act!"

"Yeah, but Vanessa didn't find it quite so funny," Sam said.

"Isn't that Kanga just the cutest?" Morgan said with a sigh.

Fiona laughed. "Morgan, you crack me up."

"We've got to get changed," Morgan told Gretta. "See you at the dance, Fe."

As they were changing out of their

cheerleading outfits, Gretta said, "I don't see why that farvann Fiona has to come with us to the dance."

"Fiona is not a farvann," Morgan told her. "She's my friend and soon to be Sam's girlfriend, from the look of things."

"But this is my first dance as a human. I just want to have some fun," Gretta whined.

"That's fine. No one is stopping you from having fun."

"It won't be any fun if Sammy's mooning over that nixie."

"Gretta—" Morgan began. But before she could say anything more, Gretta's tiny, fairy-sized cell phone rang.

"That'll be Tuti," Gretta said. "I have to go meet her to get something. Honestly, the things I do for you. If you only knew."

"What are you talking about? And why are you meeting Tuti now? You're not planning any more spells, are you? Because—"

"Trust me, Morgan, this is one time . . . oh never mind. I'll meet you back at your house." And she was gone before Morgan could stop her.

From the Journal of Gretta Fleetwing

Here I am with barely an hour left before the dance, and I am stuck, waiting to meet Tuti to get the antidote for Morgan. If Tuti doesn't hurry we will really be under a rock without a wand!

The day began well. Morgan and I went shopping and managed to find me an outfit. (Finally. I was beginning to think I'd have to go to the dance in my fairy-skins! Ha-ha!) Then we went to watch a bucket-ball game—I think that's what they call it. (Who would have thought there was a game even more boring than elf ball?) But of course I couldn't concentrate on watching the game because once again Morgan managed to get herself lost in the labyrinth, and once again it's Gretta to the rescue.

Well, it may have been a teensy bit my fault. I did make the potion after all, but I never thought that Morgan would be dumb enough to drink it! "Ah, what fools these mortals be," to quote Robin Goodfellow, a celebrity fairy. (Morgan keeps insisting that Shakespeare wrote that, but as I pointed out, Shakespeare was a mortal himself. Would he call himself a fool? I think not!)

Anyway, I had prepared a small love charm for Sammy—not that my natural charms won't do the trick, but just in case. Well, Morgan slurped it down before Sammy had a chance and immediately cast her eye on that Kanga. I've never seen a creature quite like him before! Honestly, what a ballybog. The whole thing would have been a gigantic hoot, except that we really can't have Morgan in love with a Kanga.

And poor trowling. It appears that Dog Boy is taking that jarnvidja Vanessa to the dance. I knew he was no good, and that nixie Fiona will not let Sammy out of her sight for a second. Honestly, sometimes these humans—oh! What on earth? Is that—yes, it's him. It's Bristle, hiding among the leaves above me. I will take no notice of him. As if I don't have enough on my mind right now. Hmm, where is he now? I wonder. I don't see him anymore. Has he given up so quickly? Oh there he is again.

As I was saying, the hardships I must endure. Wait—what is he doing now? Not flying home surely? No. There, I can see him again. Tuti was right about his haircut. It is definitely a big improvement. And I do like that new shirt. I must say he looks quite fetch. He has his bag with him. I wonder if he has a present for me in there. Why does he not show himself? I wonder. What kind of game is he playing? If he wants to give me a present, why can he not simply give it to me? Oh here comes Tuti. I'll tell her all about Sammy. That will make Bristle sit up and listen!

Chapter Twelve

At home Morgan took a shower and washed her hair. She wanted to look really good for Kanga.

She was blow-drying her hair, when Gretta burst into her room, out of breath and panting. "Morgan, guess what. I ran into Kanga a few minutes ago, and he asked me to give you this chocolate. He said to eat it and think of him." Gretta held out a little square of chocolate.

Morgan smiled. "Isn't he the sweetest thing? Don't you just love him?"

"I do, I do," Gretta said. "Come on, now. Down the hatch. Just like Kanga said."

Morgan popped the chocolate into her mouth and chewed. In a minute she made a face. "Are you sure he said it was chocolate?" She swallowed and said, "It tastes more like licorice, or—" Morgan stopped and stared. "Gretta?"

"What, Morgan?"

Morgan grabbed Gretta by the shoulders. "Gretta . . . tell me I did not throw myself on Kanga the Culver kangaroo in front of almost the entire school. Please tell me that did not happen."

"I wouldn't worry about it." Gretta waved her hand. "Everyone thought it was funny."

"Are you insane? We make complete fools of ourselves in front of the whole school, and you say don't worry about it?" Morgan shouted.

"Get over it, Morgan. If they noticed at all, they thought it was a hoot. You heard what Fiona said."

"She was probably just being nice. Trying to make me feel better," Morgan said.

"Everyone thought it was funny, except for that vargamor Vanessa, and who cares what she thinks?"

"I do not believe this," Morgan moaned.

"Forget about it, Morgan. Come on. Let's get ready for the dance."

"The dance? I'm not going to the dance. I

can't show my face at that school ever again. Don't you understand?"

"Well, I'm going to the dance. And right now I'm going to take a shower," Gretta said. She stomped out of Morgan's room.

Morgan sank onto her bed. This is the worst day of my life, she thought. Everyone must think I'm a total freak.

Seconds later Gretta rushed back into the bedroom and slammed the door. She yanked down the window shade. "Don't open the window and don't let him in!" Gretta shouted.

"What? Why? Let who in?" Morgan asked.

"It's Bristle. He followed Tuti and then followed me back here."

"Really?" Morgan sat up. "Where is he? Can I see him?"

"He's outside. You'll be able to see him, if he wants you to. He can't come in, unless you invite him. And you better not," Gretta warned. "This is all your fault anyway."

"My fault? What are you talking about?"

"If you hadn't drunk Sam's—oh never mind." There was a tapping on the window. "That's him! Don't let him in."

Morgan had never seen a real live elf before. She rushed to the window, and there, standing outside on the window ledge, was a tiny creature, the same one she had seen in the hand mirror. He wore baggy cargo pants, a plaid flannel shirt, and a down vest. He had a messenger bag slung over his shoulder, and a thatch of dark brown hair flopped over his forehead. He gave Morgan a friendly smile and gestured for her to open the window.

"Oh Gretta, he wants to come in," Morgan cried. "Can't we let him in?"

"No. He has no right to be here! I do not want to see him!" Gretta folded her arms across her chest and turned away from the window.

"But it's freezing out there, Gretta. And he's not dressed very warmly. He doesn't even have a coat. And no gloves."

"Whose fault is that, the dumb ballybog?" Gretta said.

Outside the elf banged on the window again. Morgan looked at him, pointed at Gretta, and shook her head. Bristle folded his hands in front of him and mouthed, "Please!"

Morgan held up a finger. "Just a minute," she mouthed to the elf.

She turned to Gretta and said, "Okay. Well look, Gretta, if you want to be ready for the dance on time, you better take your shower."

"I know, but Morgan, I'm warning you. If you let him in, you'll regret it," Gretta told her.

"I hear you. Go on. Hurry it up," Morgan said, waving her off.

Gretta went to take her shower, and as soon as Morgan heard the water running, she raced to the window and opened it. "Hi. Come on in. She's in the shower."

The elf sprang over the window ledge and landed on Morgan's desk. "Whew. Thanks, mate. It's cold as a beetle's bum out there."

Morgan nodded. "I know. I would have let you in earlier but—"

"I know," Bristle said sadly. "She doesn't want me here. But she's my girlfriend. I had to come. I—I miss her."

Morgan could tell it was hard for him to admit this. She felt sorrier than ever for him.

"I think she'll be coming back home soon,

Bristle. It won't be too much longer," she said, trying to comfort him.

He brightened. "You think?"

Morgan nodded.

"You're Morgan, right?" he asked.

"Yes. Morgan Yates."

He nodded. "She said you were nec. Guess she was right about that."

But then he frowned and narrowed his eyes. "By the way, where's that skrat she's going to the dance with? When I get my hands on him—"

"But, Bristle, she's not going with anyone," Morgan said quickly. "I mean, not like a date or anything."

"Ha! That's not what she told Tuti. I heard her. It was Sammy this and Sammy that. Yeah. Well . . ." He made fists and held them up as if to fight. "Sammy is about to become a bogtatter."

It was all Morgan could do not to laugh at the idea of this tiny fellow beating up Sam. She didn't want to insult him, though, so she said, "Look, Bristle, Sam isn't interested in Gretta. He's kind of got his eye on someone else, and—"

"Ha. Not interested in Gretta? There isn't a

guy around who's not interested in Gretta. And no wonder. She's nymphen. And, and she's funny, and—" He stopped and sat down on the edge of Morgan's math book and put his head in his hands. "She thinks I want to control her." He gave a small laugh and looked up at Morgan. "As if anyone could control Gretta."

Morgan smiled. "Not likely," she agreed.

"I don't want to control her, Morgan," he said sadly. "I just want her to come back to me."

Morgan nodded. "Look, Bristle, I'll help you; but you have to cooperate. And we can't let Gretta know I let you in. You'll have to hide, at least for now."

"I'll do whatever you say, Morgan," Bristle said.

Morgan heard the shower turn off.

"Okay. We've got to hurry! She'll be back in a minute. Get in the dollhouse for now; and whatever you do, don't let her see you or hear you, okay?"

"I'll be quiet as a pilliwigeon."

He flew to the dollhouse and went inside. Morgan threw a towel over the front so that Gretta wouldn't see in, and also so Bristle couldn't see out when they were changing.

"Pssst—Morgan?" Bristle called. "There's something you should know."

"Quiet, Bristle," Morgan hushed him. "Gretta will be back any minute."

"Well, just tell that slimy sluagh Sam that in exactly seventeen minutes, I'll be human size, and I'm gonna be looking for him."

Gretta came back from her shower and began blow-drying her hair. "Morgan, I really hope you change your mind and come. Like I said before, you need to get over yourself and stop worrying about what everyone thinks of you. You'll never make friends if you're always thinking about yourself."

"You know what, Gretta? I think you're right. I will come. I'm not nearly ready, though," Morgan told her. "But listen, I have a great idea."

"You do?" Gretta looked up.

Morgan nodded. "Hurry and get dressed, and I'll tell you."

When Gretta was dressed she spun around in a circle, admiring herself in Morgan's mirror.

"You look fantastic!" Morgan said.

"I do, don't I?" Gretta said happily. "So what's this idea of yours?"

"Come into the bathroom while I shave my legs, and I'll tell you." Morgan didn't want Bristle to hear what she was saying. "The light's better in there. You can finish putting your lipstick on."

Morgan glanced at her watch. Nine more minutes till Bristle got big. She had to make this fast.

As soon as they were in the bathroom, Morgan said, "Okay. Here's the deal. We tell Sam that I'm running late and that you arranged to meet someone at the dance. So Lorelei will drive you two there and then come back to get me."

Gretta smiled. "So Sammy and I get to ride together, just the two of us?"

"Yeah. Except for Lorelei."

Gretta clapped her hands. "I love it. Oh this is perfect!"

"Right," Morgan said.

"And so who is it I'm meeting there?" Gretta asked.

"I don't know. Anyone. It doesn't matter. Umm, gosh, you better get going." Morgan looked at her watch. Four minutes. She raced out of the bathroom and called upstairs, "Sam! Time to go. Are you ready?"

Sam came clambering downstairs, wearing his best jeans and a cool new shirt.

"You look good, Sam," Morgan told him. "New shirt?"

He smiled shyly. "You like it?"

"Absolutely!" Gretta said. "It is so fetch, Sammy!"

"Okay, let's hustle. We don't want to be late!" Morgan said, pushing both of them ahead of her down the steps.

"Lorelei? It's time for the dance. Have you got the car keys?" Morgan shouted. She hustled Sam and Gretta out of the house and into the car.

Lorelei came out a minute later. "Here I come, y'all. Just hang on."

"Look, Lorelei," Morgan said, "I'm running late, so do you mind taking them and then coming back for me?"

"It's fine with me, honey. That's what I'm here for, isn't it?"

"You're not coming with us, Morgan?" Sam asked, sounding slightly panicked.

"Sam, look at me," Morgan said. She had pulled on an old pair of jeans and a baggy sweatshirt. "I can't go like this."

"You look fine, Morgan," he said. "Come on."

"I'll be along soon," Morgan told him. She slammed the car door and ran into the house before they could stop her.

She raced upstairs and burst into her room. A human-sized Bristle was perched on the edge of her desk chair, staring at his hands in wonder. "Zeus and Apollo. Look at me. I'm as big as a gogmagog!" he said.

"Whoa!" Morgan said. "You are big, Bristle." He was at least six feet tall, taller than Sam by a few inches, and he looked very strong.

"Where's Gretta?" he asked.

"She's, uh, she's not here right now. We're going to go find her in a few minutes," Morgan told him.

He jumped up. "Is she with that wing-sapping, crown-crunching, wand-wrecking bag of lizard tongues?" he asked, his fists clenching.

"No, no, no," Morgan said quickly. "She's not with anyone like that."

"That's good, because I wouldn't want her to see what I'm going to do to him when I find him."

"By him, you mean, uh, Sam?" Morgan asked.

"Of course that's who I mean. That thistle-sticking skrat."

"Look, Bristle, let's not worry about Sam. You want to get Gretta back, right?"

Bristle slumped back down in the chair. "I do, Morgan. That's all I really want. If she would just come back to me."

Morgan got the clothes she was going to wear to the dance. "Bristle, I've got a plan. I think I know how you can get her back."

"You do?" he asked.

"I do. Just let me go get changed, and then we'll go find Gretta. You wait right here, okay?"

"Whatever you say, mate."

Morgan raced into the bathroom and changed quickly. She didn't much care how she looked. She didn't plan to stay at the dance once she got Gretta and Bristle back together. She'd made such a fool of herself already, there was no hope for her. She brushed her hair and put on some lipstick and went back to get Bristle.

From the Journal of Gretta Fleetwing

Well, this is about as much fun as riding on a porcupine! Honestly, if I'd known human dances were like this, I would have stayed home. I've been here for ages, and no one has even spoken to me. They all know each other, and I know no one, except Sammy, who hasn't paid a bit of attention to me. He didn't say a word to me the whole ride over, and that Lorelei just chatted on and on about nothing. What a gabbigammie! I tried to talk to Sammy, but he totally ignored me. The minute we got to the dance that farvann Fiona rushed up to him and dragged him off, leaving me all by myself. It's a good thing I remembered to bring my journal. At least I can benefit by doing my research, plus it gives me something to do.

And where is Morgan, by the way? Once she gets here I'll make her get Sammy to dance with me; and once that happens—well, he'll forget all about Fiona.

It is quite amusing to watch these humans, though, I must say. Poor trowlings. They dance like a bunch of bunyips!

Oops, there's my phone.

Zeus and Apollo. Tuti said that Bristle hasn't shown up for his elf-ball game and Coach is furious at him. It's one of their most important games (if elf-ball games can be considered important).

Tuti said that Jasmine the jarnvidja was crying and saying that something must have happened to Bristle because he would never not show up for a game. Since when is Bristle's schedule any of her business? I ask you!

Anyway, Tuti also said that she is worried about Bristle because he was very upset and mad when he left the kingdom. Hmm. Maybe I should have let Morgan let him in. I do wonder what has happened to him. I must admit, it is not like him to be late to an elf-ball game.

Oh look, there's Dog Boy. Hmm. I better keep my eye on him and see if he dances with the vargamor Vanessa. Oh but no. There she is over there, dancing with that other guy. Dog Boy seems to be looking for someone. Could it be Morgan? I wonder. Maybe I better go and have a little talk with him.

And where in the kingdom can Morgan be?

Chapter Thirteen

"Okay, Bristle. Let's go," Morgan said.

"You look real nice, Morgan," he said, following her downstairs.

Morgan pointed him toward the door and whispered for him to wait outside by the car. She went into the den. "Hi, Lorelei. I'm ready now. Do you mind driving me?"

"Sure thing, doll."

"We're giving my friend a ride, too. Is that okay?" Morgan shoved Bristle into the backseat and then climbed into the front next to Lorelei.

"Fine by me, hon," Lorelei told her. "You want to be dropped off at the same place I dropped Sam and Gretta?"

Bristle sat up. "Did you say Sam and Gretta?"

Uh-oh, thought Morgan.

Bristle looked at her. "I thought you told me that shaitan Sam was taking someone else to the dance?"

"That's right. I did. He is—"

"So what's he doing with my Gretta?" Bristle asked.

"Nothing. He's just, he needed a ride is all."

Lorelei said, "That Gretta sure is a talky one. She just chatted away to Sam. And Sam. He's so quietlike."

"Chatted away to Sam, did she?" Bristle asked.

"Not to Sam," Morgan said quickly. "Just chatted to, like, to anyone. You know Gretta." Morgan was babbling.

"Uh-huh. I do. And it's fine, Morgan. I'm not worried," Bristle said. He sat back and folded his arms over his chest. "I'm not worried at all."

They arrived at school, and Lorelei said, "Here we are, kids. Have fun. I'll be back for you at eleven."

"Right. Thanks, Lorelei," Morgan said. She and Bristle jumped out and started walking toward the gym. Morgan caught Bristle's sleeve. "So you—you're not worried about Sam anymore?" she asked.

Bristle shook his head calmly. "Nope," he said quietly. "Not worried a bit. Because once I get my hands on him, there won't be anything left of him to worry about." He stretched out his arms and flexed his fingers.

"Bristle, listen to me," Morgan said. She glanced around, speaking quietly so no one else would hear her. "I want to help you. I think you and Gretta should be together. But you know Gretta. You don't want her to think you're trying to control her, do you?"

He shook his head quickly. "No. I don't want her to think that."

"Right. So I've got a plan. I know it will work. But you have to trust me."

Bristle nodded.

Morgan led him behind a tree near the entrance to the gym. "Okay. Just wait right here. I'll be back for you in just a few minutes. Okay, Bristle?"

"Okay, but if that Sam comes near me, I

might have to give him a few elf bolts," he said. "And Morgan, don't make me wait too long."

"Right. Okay, Bristle. I'll be back in a jiff. Jus-just stay right here." Morgan raced inside. How was she going to keep Bristle away from Sam? As she passed the boys' locker room, she saw the Kanga suit hanging on the door. That's it, she thought. She ran into the dance. Luckily she saw Sam right away, dancing with Fiona not far from where she was. She ran up to them and said, "Sorry, Fiona, but I've got talk to Sam for a minute." She grabbed Sam by the arm and pulled him toward the hallway that led to the boys' locker room.

"Morgan, what's going on?" Sam asked.

"Sam, look. This is going to sound crazy, but something's happened, and, and, there's some-one who wants to beat you up, and—" They had reached the door to the boys' locker room. Morgan grabbed the Kanga suit and shoved it at Sam. "Here. You've got to put this on. Quick. Before he sees you."

"What? Morgan? Have you completely lost it?" he asked. "Before *who* sees me?"

"I know this sounds crazy, Sam, but you know Gretta?"

"Yeah. Your weird friend from Brooklyn or wherever."

"Yes. Right. And, well, her boyfriend is here. And he thinks you're trying to steal Gretta. He saw you with her. And now he wants to kill you."

"Her boyfriend? Is he from Brooklyn, too?" Sam asked, looking worried.

"He's from the Bronx, Sam."

"Oh."

"Just put the Kanga suit on. Fiona loves it. She'll think it's a hoot."

"The Bronx, huh? Is he big?" Sam asked.

"Huge," Morgan said.

Sam nodded, sighed, and took the Kanga suit into the locker room. Morgan ran back to the dance. She saw Gretta, sitting on the floor in a corner scribbling in her journal.

Morgan scanned the dance floor. Finally she saw her. Vanessa. She was dancing with Todd Benson. When the music stopped, Morgan rushed outside and grabbed Bristle's arm. "Come on, Bristle. You can come in now." They went into the dance, and Morgan pointed at Vanessa. "See that girl there?" she said. "Go ask her to dance," Morgan told him.

"But I don't want to dance with her," Bristle said. "I want to dance with Gretta."

"Just do it, Bristle. Trust me," Morgan told him, giving him a shove in Vanessa's direction. Bristle was bigger and older looking than most of the other guys, and he was hot. Morgan was sure Vanessa would dance with him if he asked her.

As soon as Bristle and Vanessa started dancing, Morgan raced over to Gretta.

"It's about time you got here. I don't know a soul, and that yeck Fiona won't let Sam out of her claws," Gretta complained. "But listen to this! I talked to Dog Boy and guess what—"

"Gretta, look who's dancing with Vanessa," Morgan said, pointing to Bristle and Vanessa.

Gretta stared. "Is that . . . it is! It's Bristle! He's big!"

"Definitely," Morgan said.

"And he's . . . gosh, he is fetch, isn't he. And so tall! He's even taller than Sammy," Gretta said, smiling. Then her smile faded, and her eyes narrowed. "But what is he doing with that vargamor?"

"I don't know," Morgan said. "She must think he's hot. She was all over him."

"So that gwrach thinks she can steal my boyfriend," Gretta said, stamping her foot. "Well, she has got that all wrong."

Gretta didn't wait for the music to stop. She rushed over to Vanessa and Bristle, and elbowed Vanessa out of the way.

"Excuse me, I'm dancing here," Vanessa snarled.

"Yeah, with my boyfriend!" Gretta cried. "But not for long."

"Look, you pathetic loser," Vanessa yelled. "I'll dance with whoever I want."

Bristle threw his arm around Gretta. "Hey, you can't talk to Gretta like that. No one talks to Gretta like that. Not when I'm around."

Vanessa looked from one to the other. Finally she muttered, "Whatever. You two losers deserve each other," and she stomped off.

"Did you mean it, Gretta?" Bristle asked. "I'm still your boyfriend?"

"Of course you are, you sili-ffrit!" Gretta told him. "And I better not catch you dancing with anyone else for a long time."

"Why would I dance with anyone else when I can dance with you?" he said, taking her in his arms.

Morgan smiled. Bristle looked so happy, and so did Gretta. And Sam, dressed as Kanga, had come back and was dancing with Fiona. Fiona was loving it.

Morgan was the only one who was alone. I might as well go home, she thought. No point in staying here and being miserable. She was headed toward the door when she felt a hand on her shoulder.

She looked up and saw Mr. Turner, the drama teacher. "Excuse me, Morgan," he said. "Could I talk to you for a minute?"

"Umm, sure, Mr. Turner."

"I just wanted to tell you I saw your act today, and I thought it was hilarious! I'm so pleased that you're trying out for the play!"

"My—my act?"

"Yes. You and Duncan Saunders. Duncan told me it was all improvisation. That you hadn't planned it at all. Remarkable. You're quite a comedic actress, Morgan. Have you had a lot of experience?"

"Umm." Morgan had no idea what he was talking about. Had he mixed her up with someone else? She was trying to come up with an answer when he said, "Well, I'm sure you have other things on your mind tonight, Morgan. Let's talk next week at school. I want to make sure you get the right part in the play."

"Okay. Sure."

He smiled. "I see your friend heading our way. I'll go back to my chaperoning, and you can go back to dancing!"

Morgan smiled and nodded, and Mr. Turner walked off. He had definitely mixed her up with someone else, she decided. Then she saw Duncan. He smiled and caught her hand. "Hey. I've been looking all over for you," he said.

"Y-you have?"

"Of course. You told me you'd be here, and—"

"I did?"

Duncan looked confused. "Yeah I kind of figured, I mean . . . after the game, I kind of thought . . ."

"Umm." So he had been at the game. He must think she was crazy.

"Did I misread things?" he asked sadly. "Was it just part of the act?"

Morgan was trying to figure out what he meant when Gretta rushed over. "There they are! Kanga and his partner," she said, grabbing them both by the arm. "You two were so funny out there with the cheerleaders." She squeezed Morgan's arm and gave her a look.

"Gretta, what are you talking about?" Morgan asked.

Gretta tilted her head toward Duncan. "Kanga's been looking for you, Morgan!"

Then it hit her. Finally. "Oh. Oh, right. I-I've been looking for you, too," she said, giving Duncan a huge smile. "I was, uh, a little slow getting ready."

"*Slow* is the word for it," Gretta said, rolling her eyes. "But you're both here now, aren't you, and that's all that matters."

Duncan smiled at her. "So. Should we practice our routine, or would you rather we just dance?" he asked.

He led Morgan out onto the dance floor, and they danced until the band took a break.

When they were waiting in line to get a soft drink, Duncan said, "Mr. Turner loved our routine. Did he tell you?"

"He did. He said he's really glad I'm trying out for the play," Morgan said.

"I'm glad, too. It'll be awesome," Duncan said.

"So you're going to try out?"

"Sure. I love being in plays."

"But you weren't at the meeting the other day," Morgan said.

"Mr. Turner excused me because I had to talk to Vanessa about the cheerleading routine, and try the costume on, and all that. See, the guy who usually plays Kanga is my band mate, and he asked me if I'd fill in for him." Duncan smiled and looked down at Morgan. "Tell me something," he said. "How did you know right away it was me today? It was supposed to be a big secret."

Morgan shrugged. Then she laughed and said, "My fairy godmother told me to watch out for the guy in the kangaroo suit."

From the Journal of Gretta Fleetwing

Well, unbelievable as it may seem, I am to be given no credit for flying to Morgan's side in her hour of need. These Elder Fairies just have no concept of the true nature of humans and the gallitraps they find themselves in, if left to their own devices. Thanks to me Morgan now has friends at her school, a boyfriend—yes, Dog Boy—one could wish for more, but he'll do, I suppose, and a part in the school play. She's working on the newspaper, and she's on a bicycling team. And what do I get for my efforts? They have confiscated my wand for six entire months. The unfairness of it is beyond comprehension. Oh, there's my cell phone—ooh, it's Bristle!

What a boggle-bo he is! He was calling to remind me about the game tonight, which, of course, I would never forget. Now that I'm head cheerleader, I couldn't possibly miss a game. Our cheerleading squad has been working very hard, and we have some goss cheers. I have to thank Jasmine for starting the squad. Of course it's just like her to quit the minute she realized that Bristle would never leave me for her. Poor gimil pinecone legs. It's a good thing she quit before she squashed someone!

Anyway, I better go change into my cheerleading outfit. I wish that vargamor Vanessa could see me now!

Ooh, I just had a wonderful idea. As soon as I get my wand back, I'll take Bristle with me to visit Morgan. Maybe there will be another dance we can go to! Of course silly Bristle is still jealous of Sammy, even though I've explained again and again that there was never anything between us—at least as far as my feelings were concerned. I cannot speak for Sammy, but I did sense a certain sadness about him when I said good-bye. Ah well. One cannot be to all what one would be to . . . or whatever. More later!

Gretta's Glossary of Faerish Words

baba yaga—an exceedingly ugly witch

ballybog—an elf or a type of fairy who lives in peat bogs and has a round, fat body; spindly arms and legs; and is usually covered in mud

boggle-bo—a selfish or foolish witch or goblin

bogtatter—a swamp scarecrow

bubak—a noisy house fairy who makes loud banging, pounding, and rattling noises

bunyip—a small, plump fairy whose feet are on backward

dwerg—a dwarf known for its foolishness

dwergish—foolish

fanggen—a female giant

farvann—a fairy dog

fetch—a fairy double who attracts its other; *slang*—attractive, cute, hot

gabbigammie—a tiny fairy who gibbers nonsensically; *slang*—someone who is overly chatty

gallitrap—a fairy ring caused by pixies riding horses in a circle. If you enter the ring, you will be in their power; *slang*—a bad situation

gimil—a dwarf with a limp; *slang*—lame or weak

glowergrim—one who's always worrying and grumpy

gnome-proof—easy, a cinch

gogmagog—a giant king

goss—short for *gossamer*; *slang*—cool, stylish

grak—a fire fairy who smells like rotten eggs

grakish—smelly, repulsive

gwrach—a withered hag with black teeth

hag—ugly, withered old witch or fairy

hag fit—screaming fit thrown by a hag

hag spot—ugly blemish or pimple

jarnvidja—a troll wife

nec—short for "nectar"; *slang*—sweet or cute

nellynit—a goodie-goodie

nixie—a young female water fairy who seduces young men

nixie-nocker—see above, only more so

noggle—a small, gray fairy horse; most noggles hate to get their feet wet

nymphen—beautiful

pilliwigeon—a tiny, delicate fairy who is always silent

pumphut—a house fairy who cleans and works all day

samagorska—a mountain fairy who inhabits high mountain peaks

shaitan—extremely ugly and evil

sili-ffrit—a small, childish fairy; simpleton

skrat—an evil shape-shifting ogre

sluagh—an evil troll who can change himself into a serpent

spouting—uncontrollable speaking, a common side effect of spells

trow—similar to trolls, but nicer

trowling—a trow child

vargamor—a wolf crone

yeck—a sly, mischievous, shape-shifting fairy